**"It would not do [...]
like that when [...] public
together. So, I ask again. Are you
afraid of me?"**

"No." She lifted her chin and took a step toward him. "Do you need me to prove it to you?"

Something gleamed in the depths of his eyes then, something dark and hungry, that sent a hot, electric pulse straight through her. She'd seen that gleam before, when his interest had been caught with a deal or he'd been issued a business challenge he wanted to meet. He'd never looked at her that way though, not until now, and it stole all the breath from her lungs.

That was a mistake. You've caught the attention of a predator.

She couldn't let him believe she was afraid of him, even though that might have been the safest course of action. She just couldn't. She wasn't anyone's victim.

She had caught his interest, and some long-forgotten part of her, a lost, lonely part, liked that. Liked that a lot.

Jackie Ashenden writes dark, emotional stories with alpha heroes who've just gotten the world to their liking only to have it blown apart by their kick-ass heroines. She lives in Auckland, New Zealand, with her husband, the inimitable Dr. Jax, two kids and two rats. When she's not torturing alpha males and their gutsy heroines, she can be found drinking chocolate martinis, reading anything she can lay her hands on, wasting time on social media or being forced to go mountain biking with her husband. To keep up-to-date with Jackie's new releases and other news, sign up to her newsletter at jackieashenden.com.

Books by Jackie Ashenden

Harlequin Presents

The Maid the Greek Married
His Innocent Unwrapped in Iceland
A Vow to Redeem the Greek
Spanish Marriage Solution

Three Ruthless Kings

Wed for Their Royal Heir
Her Vow to Be His Desert Queen
Pregnant with Her Royal Boss's Baby

The Teras Wedding Challenge

Enemies at the Greek Altar

Scandalous Heirs

Italian Baby Shock
The Twins That Bind

Work Wives to Billionaires' Wives

Boss's Heir Demand

Visit the Author Profile page
at Harlequin.com for more titles.

NEWLYWED ENEMIES

JACKIE ASHENDEN

PRESENTS

**Harlequin®
PRESENTS™**

ISBN-13: 978-1-335-93972-2

Newlywed Enemies

Copyright © 2025 by Jackie Ashenden

Harlequin Enterprises ULC
22 Adelaide St. West, 41st Floor
Toronto, Ontario M5H 4E3, Canada
www.Harlequin.com

Printed in Lithuania

MIX
Paper | Supporting
responsible forestry
FSC® C021394

NEWLYWED ENEMIES

A day may come where there will be a car chase in one of my books, a day of gunfights and explosions, and all the side characters, but it is not this day.

CHAPTER ONE

FLORA MCINTYRE WANTED nothing from life.

Nothing except the total ruination of Apollo Constantinides.

She stood on the other side of his vast antique oak desk—placed in lordly splendour near the window of his London office—and watched with some satisfaction as he stared at the photos she'd laid down in front of him.

They were all grainy images—she'd made sure they looked grainy—of his office, of him and her in various positions. Compromising positions. In some he had his hand on her waist, as if he was holding her, while in others he was bent over her, looking as if he was kissing her. In one she was sitting on the desk and he was crouched in front her—one stilettoed foot on his knee—while his hand cupped her bare calf, as if he was stroking it.

The images told the tale of a torrid affair they'd been having with each other, which was exactly what Flora had hoped.

Eventually, after an aeon of icy silence, Apollo lifted his head and looked at her, his dark green eyes blazing with barely contained fury. 'Where did these come from?'

He was the most coldly controlled man she'd ever met, so for him to betray anger meant he was truly in a titanic rage.

How satisfying.

Flora schooled her expression to show nothing but concern. 'I was sent them anonymously.'

Apollo looked back down at them for a moment, muttered a curse, shoved back his chair and stood. He turned his back on her, staring out the windows to the London skyline beyond.

It had taken her six months of careful planning to get the photos, and then another couple of weeks to choose the ones that looked the most incriminating. The ones that would appear to indicate that Apollo Constantinides—billionaire investor, Nobel-nominated, well-known philanthropist, winner of various awards for his ethical business practices, including landmark sexual harassment policies—was having an affair. With his PA.

Apollo Constantinides, who'd just got engaged to Violet Standish, head of a global charity aimed at helping women who had survived such crimes as domestic violence, sexual violence, trafficking and drug abuse. Violet's charity had won awards, too, and the news of their engagement had been the subject of much positive press.

Sadly for Apollo, Flora had just torpedoed said engagement, and she didn't feel a single shred of regret about it. Especially when she knew for a fact that it wasn't a love match, but a business arrangement. In fact, Flora had often wondered if Apollo was even capable of such a soft emotion as love.

He was a hard man, blunt to the point of offensiveness—his commitment to honesty was total. He was also cold, ruthless and utterly determined to get what he wanted. Really, she was doing Violet Standish a favour, even if the engagement was purely for strategic business reasons. Violet would soon learn that she'd married a shark, not a man, and Flora wouldn't wish that on her own worst enemy.

She glanced down at the photos again and gave herself a mental pat on the back.

The photos were all part of the plan she'd put into motion years ago, after her beloved father, David, had taken his own life, having lost everything in an infamous Ponzi scheme run by Apollo's own father, Stavros Constantinides.

That Stavros had been sent to jail and died there wasn't justice enough for Flora. Not for the pain her mother, Laura, had endured, after David had selfishly taken the easy way out. Not for the years of living on the poverty line, because her mother had refused all offers of compensation, calling it 'blood money'. Not for how she'd been left alone—physically, due to the two jobs Laura had to take on, and emotionally, due to her mother's grief. Laura had eventually died of cancer far too young. Cancer she'd ignored the signs of because she was too tired and too broken to care about her own health.

Not for the powerlessness Flora had felt after her father's suicide, then watching her mother slowly get sicker and sicker, knowing there was nothing she could do to help her.

Not for a life bled dry of hope, happiness and the promise of a better future.

No. The only justice for Flora was the total and complete annihilation of everything Apollo Constantinides cared about.

Because while Stavros might be dead, his son was still alive, and his son was the man who'd convinced Flora's father to invest in Stavros's scheme in the first place. It didn't matter that Apollo had turned his father in. It didn't matter that subsequently he'd given compensation to all those affected by the scheme, and then tried to rehabilitate the family name with his ethical business practices, and philanthropic donations. It didn't matter that he and Violet had been jointly nominated for a Nobel Peace Prize, for their charitable work in human rights and, most importantly, the rights of women globally.

As far as Flora was concerned, the only thing that mattered was never feeling that sense of powerlessness, of helplessness, ever again. And she would do that by channelling every ounce of her rage into making sure Apollo lost everything. His engagement to Violet would be the first casualty.

Flora stood quietly before his desk, watching his tall, powerful form as he directed the full force of his fury to the cityscape beyond the glass, and allowed herself a small, private smile.

She'd spent three years at Helios Investments, his investment company, initially as a junior secretary in the HR department, before steadily working her way up the chain, until she'd finally landed the position she'd been aiming for. Apollo's PA.

She'd been in that position for a year now, gaining his trust, making herself indispensable. He had no knowledge of her links to Stavros's scheme. He didn't know who she was—her parents hadn't been legally married, so she'd kept her mother's name as her own legal surname—and she'd make sure he never would.

Hiding those links hadn't been difficult, despite him being a very sharp, astute and intelligent man. After all, no one was particularly interested in the family history of one of his employees, even if that employee was his personal PA. She'd passed all the stringent background checks he ran on all his staff, signed the NDAs that were mandatory, and no one had said anything to her.

It had been easy.

There was, however, one small problem with Apollo Constantinides. One teeny, tiny issue she'd never completely managed to solve. And that was the fact that he was literally the hottest man she'd ever had the misfortune of meeting, and every time he got close—every time he even looked at her—her heart would beat fast and her mouth would go dry.

She hated it.

She hated his beauty.

She hated him.

Six foot three, with short black hair. Eyes the colour of a deep, dark jungle, with winged soot-black brows. A straight nose that harkened back to his Greek heritage, and a mouth that haunted her dreams. He was also intensely charismatic, with the sort of authority that made emperors kneel. He held the whole world in the palm of his hand and he knew it.

And that had made every one of those compromising photos she'd taken an enormous trial, because of how near she had to get to him. It had been a test of both her resolve and her ability to dissemble, but she'd aced it, if she did say so herself.

Not that there was any doubt. Working with him as closely as she did was its own form of exposure therapy and, after those photos, she could safely say she was now fully inoculated.

Apollo turned abruptly from the window and, despite herself, despite all her bracing thoughts of how impervious she was to him, her breath caught as she was pinned by his intense green gaze.

He was in her favourite suit today—dark grey wool, tailored perfectly to his powerful figure—and a plain white shirt. His silk tie was a myriad of different greens, reflecting the colour of his eyes.

'This is unacceptable,' he said, his normally cool, deep voice hot with leashed anger. 'I want a full investigation as to where they came from.'

Flora made sure none of her considerable satisfaction showed. 'Don't worry,' she said smoothly. 'I already have that in hand.'

'What about online? Have the pictures reached the wider public yet?'

'I have the tech department looking into that right now.' She adjusted her expression, so it showed the appropriate amount of concern. 'Unfortunately I think some of them have made their way into online spaces.' And they had. She'd posted them on various platforms herself. 'And once it's out on the web...'

A muscle in the side of Apollo's impressive jaw twitched. 'Get IT onto it. I want the pictures taken down. All of them. Immediately.' He turned back to the desk again. 'How is this even possible?' He leaned forward, hands gripping the edge of the desk, staring at the photos as if he was trying to light them on fire with the power of his mind alone. Which, given his ruthless determination when he wanted something, could very well happen. 'These were taken in this office.'

'It seems so,' Flora said carefully. 'Perhaps they used a telephoto lens or planted a small camera somewhere. Those things are pretty small these—'

'What are people saying?' His gaze came to hers once more, a laser focus that always managed to steal her breath away. 'What about the media? What's PR doing?'

He did not, she noted, ask how she felt, which, considering she was also in the photos, was yet another black mark against his name.

'I've informed them.' She kept her tone cool and controlled. 'I also made sure they knew that, despite the photos, there is nothing going on between us.'

And there wasn't. Apollo was a model employer. He'd never crossed any boundaries with her, never betrayed the slightest hint that he was even aware she was a woman, let alone anything else.

It was almost disappointing in a way. Ever since she'd

started work at Helios, she'd been looking for hard evidence that he was the same man who'd convinced her father to buy into Stavros' scheme, yet she hadn't found any. That didn't mean it wasn't there though.

David had always been looking for get-rich-quick shortcuts, and had been convinced by Apollo that Stavros's investment scheme was legitimate, no matter how much it had looked too good to be true.

But then that was Apollo Constantinides. He'd made an art out of looking too good to be true. When his father had gone to jail, Apollo had somehow avoided a sentence himself. He'd acted contrite in the interviews he'd given in the news media. Portraying himself as also a victim of his father's lies, garnering sympathy with his blunt honesty and his willingness to offer compensation.

Flora knew the truth though. The only thing he really cared about was his reputation, and that was it. People were there to either be used to help polish that reputation or they were seen as hindrances and got rid of. She'd personally seen him fire a man who'd been using the company credit card to pay for a few little treats of his family. It had been wrong, yes, but the amounts of money spent had been small, and the man had confessed. In fact, he'd pleaded with Apollo to let him stay, but Apollo had fired him with the same cold indifference with which he treated most people.

'There is nothing going on between us whatsoever,' Apollo agreed, glancing down at the photos scattered over his desk, dark brows drawing down into a scowl. 'Inform Violet,' he added. 'She needs to—'

He broke off abruptly, dug into his pocket and pulled out his phone. His scowl deepened as glanced at the screen, but he hit the answer button all the same. 'Violet.' His tone softened as he said her name. 'Yes, I've seen the pictures. You must know that Flora and I have nothing to do—' He stopped, sent a furious glance at Flora, before turning to the windows once again. 'What?' he asked.

Flora moved over to the desk and began to gather the pictures up slowly, keeping half an ear on the conversation with Violet.

'I realise what people will say,' Apollo was murmuring. 'But my PR department is excellent, you know that. It'll all blow over and… Yes, I understand the media is harder on women. Which is why I'll… What?' He was silent, but Flora could feel the rage emanating from him like an icy breeze straight off a glacier. 'We can change the optics,' he went on after a moment. 'You can't possibly let this—'

Flora stole a glance at him.

He stood gazing out of the windows, his face in profile, as perfect as that of a king on a coin. But that muscle jumped again in the side of his jaw.

'Yes,' he bit out, his tone now icy. 'I see. Well naturally I wouldn't want anything to compromise the integrity of your business… Fine. Will you let me do the honourable thing at least? You can play up the part of being the wronged woman. Yes… Yes… Good. I'll send over the press release beforehand.'

Flora couldn't resist another private smile. Sounded as if Violet was breaking things off, which was exactly

what she'd hoped. The world needed to see just how cold
and ruthless he was, and she would expose him.

She'd make the world see the truth about Apollo Constantinides if it was the last thing that she did.

Apollo couldn't believe it.

Violet had broken off their engagement.

Their wedding was supposed to be the icing on the
cake, the crowning achievement of all the work he'd put
into rehabilitating the Constantinides name. Marriage to
Violet Standish, head of one of the world's leading philanthropic institutions, was going to be the perfect union
of two pillars of the global community.

When they'd announced their engagement—after the
NDAs and other contracts had been signed, naturally—
the press had had a field day. His PR department had
told him that faith in the Constantinides name had never
been so high and Helios's stocks were through the roof.
Everyone was totally for their 'ship', sharing opinions
and photos and memes on every internet platform there
was. Apollo had been thoroughly satisfied with the optics. He hadn't even minded the press calling their part-
nership 'ViLo'.

But now…

Violet had been adamant that their union could not
possibly go ahead. Associating herself with a 'cheater'
would irreparably damage her charity's brand, and considering it was a charity dedicated to helping women
from all walks of life and in different situations, he
couldn't blame her.

Except right now, he very much wanted *someone* to blame.

And then that someone to *pay*.

His jaw ached from clenching it, all his muscles tight with fury. He didn't know how those pictures had been taken from inside his office—someone must have sneaked in a camera somehow—but all of those images were totally innocent. The strap on Flora's shoe had broken, so he'd told her to sit on the desk. Then he'd kneeled in front of her to try and fix it, that was all. His hand cupping her calf was to steady her because she'd been ticklish, it had *not* been a caress.

Then, that one of him sitting back in his chair while she bent over him... She'd said there had been a spot on his shirt, and he'd let her double check the cotton was clean, because he'd been busy talking on the phone.

All the pictures looked compromising, yes, but they weren't. He hadn't touched her like *that*, and he never would.

Someone had set him up.

Apollo bit back the growl that formed in his throat as he furiously went over possibilities. An employee with a grudge? Could be. He was a demanding boss, and plenty of people didn't like that, even though they were paid handsomely for it. A spurned lover? Probably not. He hadn't indulged in lovers since his engagement, and even before that he only slept with women who wanted what he did—sex and nothing more.

A business rival? That was very possible. Helios was,

after all, a global company, and there were those who still remembered his father transgressions.

Not that the question of who or even why mattered in the greater scheme of things.

He'd worked too hard, for too long retrieving the Constantinides name from the gutter his father had thrown it in, and he wasn't going to let some nameless fool use clumsily staged photos to throw it back.

Taking a couple of silent breaths to get his fury under control, he turned from the window.

Flora was gathering up the photos on his desk with careful hands, her expression, as usual, impassive. Over the year he'd had her as his PA, he'd found her not only to be cool, calm, collected, but also extremely competent. An excellent employee, who never complained about the amount of work he gave her—and it was a lot of work, he was a very busy man.

Today she was in her normal PA uniform of a plain black pencil skirt and plain white blouse, buttoned all the way up. Her black hair was smooth and sleek, coiled into a neat bun on the top of her head, and she radiated no-nonsense competence. He'd never seen her with a hair out of place or look flustered in any way. She was as serene as a swan, the best PA he'd ever had.

Even now, even with those pictures of herself in all those positions, she seemed unflappable. No doubt she'd weather it with her usual calm.

It was different for him. He had more to lose than she did.

'We will need to draft and send a press release,' he bit out. 'Violet has called off the engagement.'

No expression of shock moved over Flora's delicate features. She was, as ever, perfectly composed. 'I'm sorry to hear that, sir,' she said. 'How quickly will you need a draft?'

She'd always called him 'sir', even though he'd never insisted. It had never bothered him, but today, for some reason, it got under his skin, as did her entire cool manner.

Wasn't she concerned about those pictures? Didn't it matter to her? Not even for her own sake?

'As soon as possible.' He kept rigid control over his own tone and expression. It would not do to betray just how furious he was. His emotions were kept under lock and key; as he'd learned, there was no room for them in business. 'You do not seem unduly concerned, Flora,' he noted coolly. 'And you should be. This is a serious problem, and it involves you.'

'Yes, I understand that, sir.' She gave an elegant little shrug. 'But there's not much I can do about it. The photos are in the public arena and it will be next to impossible to get them all taken down.'

Again, she said it all with zero emphasis, as if her own reputation and his good name were of no importance to her.

'I don't care how impossible or otherwise it is,' he snapped icily, trying to keep the lid on his temper. 'I want them gone.'

'Of course, sir,' she murmured, long black lashes veiling her gaze.

Was she placating him? If so, that was a mistake. He hated being managed. 'I will not have the Constantinides name dragged in the mud,' he said, insistent. 'I want whoever is responsible for these pictures found.'

'Naturally, sir.' She collected the photos into a neat little stack, then began sliding them back into their envelope.

Every moment was precise, calm and controlled, and for some reason he found that extremely aggravating. 'Leave them,' he snapped. 'I will be handing them on to the police.'

'I'm quite happy to—'

'No, I will do it.' He really was having difficulty keeping the annoyance from his voice, which was concerning. Normally he had no problems mastering himself. Then again, the potential crumbling of the Constantinides good name was not a normal situation. 'Since the pictures concern you and I,' he continued, 'we'll need an explanation for them as soon as possible. Now, in fact. Violet and I have agreed that I will break off the engagement, and I won't have her waiting.'

Flora's eyes, the dark charcoal grey of river stones, gave nothing away. 'What do you suggest regarding explanations?'

'Denial will only stir up more fuss.' Which was true. He'd observed that when his father's investment scheme had collapsed. Stavros had kept up his protestations of innocence, that the scheme was perfectly legitimate, all the way to court—and then all the way to jail. It had made the media circus of the trial more intense, the sensational suicide of one of his victims adding more fuel to the fire.

Apollo would not make the same mistake. He was adept at manipulating his public image—he'd learned in a hard school after all—and the best way to deal with a media blaze was to deprive it of oxygen. Either that, or encourage the wind to turn, so the flames burned in the opposite direction.

Unfortunately, Flora was likely correct, the pictures would be impossible to take out of circulation, and attempting to do so now would only make things worse. No, the only way to play this was to not deny what the photos implied, but to take the speculation and turn it on its head.

That meant he'd have to admit that he and Flora *were* in fact involved. It would be a complete and total fabrication, which went against everything he believed in, but there was no help for it. His reputation and that of his company was more important. Helios was supposed to be a model employer, and it would not do to look as if he'd thrown one of his own employees under the bus. Which meant protecting Flora from any blowback was also vital.

So, how to make all of this sympathetic? He couldn't say it was a passing affair, that wouldn't help his cause, especially since he was her boss. His rigorous sexual harassment policies had been lauded around the globe as an example of new, progressive business practices, and having such an obvious affair would label him a hypocrite.

He couldn't stand that. He'd never crossed the line with his employees and never would, and he believed totally in those policies. He'd drafted them himself.

However, there might be those who didn't like his management style, who might see this as an opportunity to take him down peg or two. They might use it as an example of his behaviour to bring spurious claims against him.

So, no affair then. He'd have to claim that Flora was something more than merely his PA, and that their affair was more than merely an affair. It would have to be a grand passion, a meeting of soulmates, or something along those lines. All nonsense, of course. Love was a vice he'd never be guilty of, but it was the best way to save the Constantinides name.

People loved a romance, they were gullible like that, as he would know, since his father had taught him all about how gullible people were. How to prey on their little weaknesses, their little vulnerabilities, and turn them to his advantage. It wasn't manipulation, he'd told Apollo. It was merely business, and where business was concerned anything was allowed.

Of course, he'd soon learned that his father's 'lessons' were nothing but Stavros manipulating his own son, but Apollo had learned them all the same.

Now, though, he went still, as his brain offered him a solution that would allow Flora and himself a modicum of respectability, not to mention a way out for Violet also. A way that would limit the damage of the pictures as much as possible. It wasn't the most elegant of solutions, since it would involve a lie. But it was a harmless lie, which would hurt no one and, most importantly, would potentially rescue the Constantinides name.

'Then what else do you suggest?' Flora asked, her expression still unruffled.

'I suggest that we don't deny it,' he said, holding her gaze. 'In fact, I think the perfect solution is for me to marry you instead of Violet.'

CHAPTER TWO

AT FIRST FLORA thought she'd misunderstood him, because seriously, marriage? To *her*? Was he insane?

Then, when the intense laser beam of his focus didn't relent, the lines of his perfect face unyielding, she understood that, yes, he was serious. And, no, he likely wasn't insane.

The idea was so preposterous, though, she almost laughed. So near to almost, in fact, she could feel her mouth begin to curl into a smile without her express permission. Which was not acceptable. She *had* to be on her guard with him.

She'd managed to get away with the photos only because he treated her as an extension of himself, and so didn't pay much attention to her specifically. Which was exactly what she wanted.

What she did not want was him looking at her the way he was doing so now, as if he was a scientist and she an interesting specimen he was examining through a microscope.

He couldn't be interested in her. He couldn't be curious about her. Because, if he looked too closely, he might find out who she really was and she couldn't allow that to happen. She had to be as unexceptional and boring as possible.

Forcing her shock aside, Flora tried to maintain her usual calm manner. 'I don't understand. How is marrying me a solution?'

Apollo came back to his desk and stood behind it, suddenly seeming much too tall and much too powerful for her comfort. She hated how sometimes her awareness would zero in on him, noting all the things about him that she liked. It was all physical—her body was inexplicably drawn to his in a way that she couldn't seem to shake off.

Even now, at the point of achieving the first step in her revenge plans, she couldn't help but notice the breadth of his wide shoulders and chest. The light coming in through the windows behind him and turning his black hair glossy, shadowing the hard planes and angles of his face. The deep jungle green of his eyes, glittering like dark emeralds.

He was the most physically perfect man she'd ever met, and if he was any other man she'd be dazzled. But he wasn't any other man, he was the man who'd destroyed her family, and the only thing that should dazzle her was her own genius at managing to stay hidden from him all this time.

'As I mentioned,' he said, 'denial will only make the situation worse, as will ignoring the issue. Admitting that we're having an affair is our only option.'

Which was not what Flora had been expecting. At all. His anger was right on target, but she'd thought the damage control would be denial. He hated a lie, and she'd counted on his outrage at being accused of something he hadn't done to dig in and, yes, that *would* make things worse. She wanted it to be worse.

The last thing she'd anticipated was him deciding to embrace the lie.

'W-what?' she said, unable to help the slight stutter.

His gaze pinned her to the spot, sharp needles of green glass holding her in place. 'We admit that we've been seeing each other. We won't call it an affair, though, as that implies something casual and sordid, so we'll have to go with calling it a grand passion instead. One that we tried to resist and failed, and then I ended up asking you to marry me and, naturally, you said yes.'

Flora blinked as her brain tried to get a handle on what he was saying. Not an affair, but a grand passion that ended in a marriage proposal?

The calm, which came with feeling totally in control of the situation she'd engineered, began to dissipate, and that could not happen.

She was going to have to recalibrate her entire plan.

'I see,' she managed.

'You have doubts?' His deep voice carried the familiar tone of faint impatience, which he used whenever someone questioned him. 'This will mitigate the damage of the photos, and perhaps even garner some public sympathy, especially if it looks like we're desperately in love with each other. It will also allow Violet an opportunity to be magnanimous and noble in allowing us our happiness.'

He wasn't wrong—even she could see that. It would allow everyone some dignity, a dignity that she'd been counting on him *not* having.

You should have expected him to come up with the perfect solution. He's far too smart not to.

Yes, she should have, damn him. Her intentions had been to set him on the back foot, not herself.

Flora tried to moisten her suddenly dry mouth. 'We're not in love with each other, though,' she said, the statement more to buy herself some time to think than any kind of protest.

His black brows twitched. 'No, of course we aren't. This isn't about reality, Flora. It's about optics.' Alarmingly, he rounded the desk and headed straight for her, and it was all she could do not to take a step back. Getting close to him was always an issue since it was difficult to disguise her physical reaction to his nearness, just as it was difficult to think clearly. Yet she couldn't give ground. He would note it and wonder why, and he was already asking too many questions as it was. Allowing him to ask more would be a mistake.

He was a man who took charge of any given situation, and if she wasn't careful he was going to take charge of this too.

She couldn't let that happen. She had to act before he did.

Flora held her ground as he came to a stop just in front of her, tilting her head back so she could meet his intent green gaze. 'Of course, sir,' she said with a calm she didn't feel. 'Optics are important.'

'Indeed,' he said. 'In which case we will need to be seen in public together. You will also need a ring. The wedding will have to be a circus, there's no escaping that, but if it's big enough people will soon forget about those photos.'

He was far too close for comfort, his nearness making her thoughts feel like they were coated in warm honey, slow and thick. The warm, woody scent of his after-shave was the most delicious thing she'd ever smelled, and she had the almost overwhelming urge to lean in and inhale him.

'We can stay married for six months,' he went on. 'Or perhaps a year. Then we'll get a divorce once all the fuss has died down. No harm done.'

Get it together, fool! You can't go sniffing him when he's in the middle of ruining your revenge plans!

'Well? Are you listening, Flora?'

Flora gritted her teeth and wrestled her recalcitrant awareness back into submission. What had he been talking about again? A ring. A wedding. They can stay married for six months, a year…divorce.

He is *taking charge of this, and you're letting him.*

'Yes, I heard you,' she said, by now holding on to the calm by the skin of her teeth. 'A ring and a wedding. Divorce. This will all be just for show, I hope?'

Apollo's dark brows twitched again. 'It will be a paper marriage, naturally, but from a legal standpoint it will be absolutely real. I abhor a lie, Flora, you know this.'

'Yes, I do know that, actually.' The words escaped without her conscious control, as did the edge of sarcasm.

His gaze narrowed. 'You don't seem to be treating this situation with the appropriate amount of concern.'

Damn him. And damn herself for letting him get under her skin so badly. This attraction to him was a problem, and she should have found a solution by now. She'd hoped that ignoring it would make it go away, yet it hadn't. If anything, it seemed to have got worse.

It was stupid. She'd basically ignored men in her quest to get herself to where she was now, and that had been made easier since she'd never met a man she wanted. Now, though, it seemed some kind of karmic joke that the one man who'd ever affected her was the one man she hated, who she hoped to bring down.

Ugh.

'I'm very concerned.' She kept her tone cool. 'But surely we don't have to go through with an actual marriage. You can break up with me or something—'

'No.' The word was hard and flat, the weight of his authority turning it into an anvil dropped from a great height. 'It will be a pretence both emotionally and physically, but legally it must be real. I will not have it discovered later that the whole thing is a lie.'

Great. There went the idea of her leaking a pretend marriage to the press.

'No, of course not,' she said soothingly.

He frowned down at her. 'Don't placate me, Flora, I won't have it. Just as I won't have the Constantinides name attached to some sordid headline or nonsense soap opera. These photos, wherever they came from, are likely a setup, and I will not be held to ransom by them.'

Of course he'd already thought this through. And once again, she should have anticipated that he'd move quickly and decisively. He'd never been a man to sit around wringing his hands when faced with a seemingly insoluble problem, after all. He made decisions and took action.

God, why couldn't he have been more of a wet blanket?

'I'm not placating you, sir,' she said, adjusting her tone a touch. 'I actually agree with you. Denial would look bad, and it would likely only encourage more gossip. Perhaps, though, an actual wedding would be overkill?'

Apollo's gaze became intent in a way she wasn't expecting. 'Why? What does it matter to you whether the marriage is real or not?'

Her heart thudded, suddenly loud in her ears, and for no reason that she could see. He did this sometimes, turn his attention onto her like a predator spotting prey, and it always made her breath catch and her adrenaline spike.

She'd been so careful the whole year she'd been working for him, always appearing calm and cool and in control. Never questioning him. Never talking about herself. Never doing anything that would draw his attention. She'd been so pleased with herself at the way she'd managed to keep hold of all her secrets, that perhaps she'd become complacent.

'It doesn't matter to me,' she said carefully. 'But... Well. I might be seeing someone, or have a partner.'

He didn't even blink. 'And are you? Seeing someone, I mean.'

'No, but...'

'But what?'

'What about the expense? A real wedding is a waste of money.'

'I don't care about the expense.' He frowned down at her. 'I'm trying to protect you as well, Flora. You do see that, don't you? I'm your boss, don't forget. Which makes the optics on this whole situation look even worse, especially since Helios is supposed to be a world leader when it comes to employee relations. Then there's the Constantinides name to consider, and I will not put that reputation in jeopardy. Which means this has to be as real as it humanly can be.' He folded his arms across his broad chest. 'It will be better for both of us if it looks like a passionate public love affair and ends with a fairy-tale wedding. That will make the public forget there were even photos of us in the first place.'

Oh, he was clever. She really, *really* should have known he'd find some way to spin this, even that bit about protecting her. He was wasted as a CEO. He should have gone into politics instead, since he had the power to make even the devil himself look good.

Perhaps the photos were a stupid idea. You should have just gone with the insider trading stuff.

The photos, of course, weren't the whole of her plan. She had a bullet-point list of all the things she was going to do to ensure his total and utter destruction, only one of which involved incriminating photos. Aiming at the monolith of his personal reputation was the first of her targets and the easiest one to undermine—at least that's what she'd thought when she'd first taken the job as his PA.

She'd considered a seduction initially, but then had discarded the idea, since he seemed to be an entirely passionless man, and she certainly wasn't experienced enough to generate any kind of response from him, despite the response he managed to generate in her. So, she'd gone with engineered photos instead.

You were far too satisfied, far too soon.

Yes, she had been. And now the damage control she had to undertake was for her own plans, which had suddenly become a whole lot more complicated.

It wasn't insurmountable, however. She could still salvage things. She had to keep her cool, stay in control and not betray just how badly he'd rattled her.

'Very well,' she said with what she thought was admirable calm. 'Shall I add all this to the draft press release or would you like to do it?'

Flora gazed back at him, one dark brow arched in polite enquiry, and he found it…irritating. Normally her calm and unflustered manner was the thing he appreciated most about her as a PA, but not today. Especially when he was seething inside that someone had dared think they could try to ruin him, because that's clearly what was happening.

It wouldn't work, though. He'd make sure of that. He'd turn around and marry the woman they'd used to try and ruin him, and he'd come out of the whole affair smelling like roses.

Violet wouldn't mind. He'd entered into a marriage agreement with her initially for the cachet her name would bring to him and to Helios, and also to add a further layer of insulation for the precious crystal that was the Constantinides reputation. His father had shattered it into glittering shards, but Apollo would put it back together, piece by piece, if it was the last thing he did.

It wasn't purely for his own sake. He had thousands of employees around the globe who would lose their jobs if Helios collapsed, as well as all the charities that benefited from his money. And last, but certainly not least, for the memory of his mother, Elena, who'd believed totally in Stavros, and who'd been left heartbroken after Stavros had gone to jail.

She'd died a few years ago of complications due to pneumonia, and the last words she'd ever spoken to him had been to request that he rebuild the family name. She'd left unsaid the role he'd played in his father's downfall, yet he'd heard her loud and clear all the same.

This was all your fault...

She was wrong, of course. His father's scheme had been doomed from the start, and someone would have turned him in eventually. That it had been his son was something neither of his parents had been able to get over, but that had been their problem, not his.

Yes, he'd told the police about his father. Yes, he'd turned Stavros in.

He'd gained immunity from prosecution in return, but that wasn't why he'd done it. He'd done it because a man had died after hearing the scheme was illegal—a man Apollo himself had brought on board, and turning Stavros in had been the right thing to do. He hadn't felt guilty about sending his father to jail, not then and not now, not one single shred. Not when his father hadn't felt guilty about all the people he'd been duping, and all the lives he'd destroyed.

Stavros had sold it to Apollo as some kind of glorified Robin Hood scheme, that what they were doing was merely taking from the rich and giving to the poor. Apollo had loved his father, and working in the family company was all he'd ever wanted to do. However, that love had blinded him to the truth. It hadn't been an enterprise to invest money in new tech that would allow impoverished communities to access clean water and cheap power. It had been a scheme that allowed Stavros to take all the investors' money for himself to clear his own debt.

His father had told him, just before they'd locked him away, that all he'd wanted was to make sure the company survived for Apollo and Elena's sake. He didn't say anything about how his own financial mismanagement had run Helios into the ground and he had no one to blame for his jail sentence but himself.

Which was why Apollo had decided, early on, that the only way he could mitigate the damage his father had caused was to get Helios back on its feet again, and make it as profitable as he could, so he could then offer his father's victims some decent compensation.

Luckily, he had a gift when it came to finance and investing, but, even so, it had taken a lot of hard work and determination to earn back the trust Helios had commanded before his father had ruined it, and then more work to get it making money again.

At that stage, though, he'd realised that nothing less than the total and complete rehabilitation of the Constantinides name would do. That not only was compensation for the victims not enough, but spearheading a movement to overhaul company business practices worldwide, especially when it came to protecting staff, was also necessary.

There were ways to be ethical and honest when it came to investing. There were ways to be transparent. There were ways to prioritise people's wellbeing that didn't impact the bottom line, and, in fact, you could have both.

He didn't want anyone else falling for charlatans like his father either, so he'd dedicated one arm of Helios to investigating and exposing Ponzi schemes and other illegal, unethical business practices. He also gave away a significant portion of his wealth. He was what his father wasn't, a true Robin Hood. Taking from the rich—himself—and giving it to those desperately in need.

He was also not a man who compromised, and he would not compromise on this. Just as he would not compromise on ways to scupper the plans of whoever it was who was trying to ruin him.

He had, however, expected more objections from Flora.

She'd seemed shocked at his initial suggestion—he'd definitely caught a flicker of it in her eyes, which was of note, since she was always unflappable. Then his curiosity had been further engaged when she'd protested the idea of them having a real marriage.

She'd never questioned one of his decisions, not once, and he'd accepted that, because he was of the view that a PA should make everything he did smoother and easier, not more difficult, with lots of questions. He had other people to do that kind of thing and she was not one of them.

He'd never wanted to know her as a person or have her tell him details about her life. He wasn't interested.

Yet, now, he found himself intrigued by the fact that, out of all the decisions he'd made since she started working for him, she'd been so unusually vocal about this one. He wanted it to be a legal marriage, yes, but only on paper, nothing more, so what was really the issue here?

Did she think he meant it? Did she think that he really felt something for her? Or was it something else?

He took a moment to study her.

She wasn't beautiful, not typically so, though her face was possessed of a certain…interest. And her PA uniform did accentuate a lush, womanly figure, which wasn't perhaps fashionable, but now that he was looking it was…well, again, interesting.

But he shouldn't be looking, not when he was her boss. He liked to lead by example, and whoever had set him up had known that, since they were hitting him where it would do the most damage.

Colour had risen to her cheeks, which was odd. He'd looked at her a thousand times like this and she'd never blushed before, or at least not that he'd noticed. Had it been the mention of a grand passion between them? Had it embarrassed her? Or was she merely uncomfortable being studied?

Why are you even being curious about her? She's just your PA.

This was true, he'd never been curious about her before. He needed to stop.

'You can add it to the draft,' he said after a moment. 'But first, we'll need to agree on what story we give to the press about our love affair.'

She nodded calmly. 'As you said before, we met at work, obviously. And after a few months of working together—perhaps after a few late-night strategy sessions?—we gradually realised our love for one another.'

The whole sentence was delivered in the same dispassionate tone with which she delivered everything she said. Which would not do, not if they were going to act as if they were the love of each other's lives.

He gave her a severe look. 'We're supposed to be talking about irresistible passion, Flora, not giving a PowerPoint presentation.'

Again, there was that flicker in her eyes, and the dark brow she had arched, arched further. 'Oh? I didn't realise we had to fully enact our irresistible passion right now.'

Apollo narrowed his gaze at the faint hint of sarcasm in her voice.

He was adept at reading people—it was what his father had taken advantage of, back when Apollo had been younger and still thinking that his father's idea for an investment scheme was a marvellous opportunity. He'd been the public face of the scheme, had read the files of all the potential investors his father had sent his way, noting any frailties or vulnerabilities. He'd enjoyed showing off his gift to Stavros as much as Stavros had enjoyed using it.

Even these days, even though he knew where it had the potential to lead, he'd found himself using it to his own advantage in the boardroom. Though—and he had to remember this—it was all in service to furthering good in the world rather than duping people. He wasn't like his father. He wasn't.

'This is not a game,' he said repressively. 'This is about Helios's reputation, and the thousands of people we employ. I am this company, and if I fall, so does everyone else.'

If she was chastened by this, she gave no sign, except for a minute tightening of her full lips. 'Very well. How else would you like me to talk about it then?'

He ignored the question for a moment, caught by that almost imperceptible sign of annoyance. Was she angry with him? Or was it the photos? She hadn't seemed upset by them, and yet surely she had to be.

'You don't seem put out by these photos.' He met her steady stare, noting another flicker deep in the charcoal depths of her eyes. What was it? Another emotional response? And if so, why was she hiding it?

Her lashes fell, veiling her gaze. They were thick, those lashes, and a deep, sooty black. He couldn't recall noticing them before, and wasn't sure why he was noticing them now.

'I'm startled by them,' she said evenly. 'But they're in the public domain now. There's nothing I can do about it.'

'And you really don't know who sent them to you?' he asked, noting yet another tightening of her lips. 'Or do you have any idea who might have?'

Her gaze remained veiled, which he found frustrating. He didn't like not being able to read people. It made him feel as if something was being hidden from him, and he didn't like that either. He wasn't the gullible fool he'd been back at twenty, when he'd thought everything his father said was the God's honest truth. These days he questioned everything.

Reaching out, he put a finger beneath Flora's determined chin and tilted her head back. 'You know something about them, don't you?' His fingers closed on her warm skin. 'Tell me, Flora.'

CHAPTER THREE

FLORA'S BREATH CAUGHT abruptly, every inch of skin pulling tight. She couldn't seem to move, all her awareness zeroing in on the firm press of his long fingers holding her chin. Warm and strong. She had the impression that, even if she'd wanted to, she wouldn't have been able to pull away.

His gaze pinned her to the spot and she realised that his eyes weren't the simple dark green she'd always thought they were. It was as if someone had taken an emerald and shattered it, with some of the pieces glittering a lighter, grass green, while others were darker, spruce and pine. Many shades, like his tie, and all perfectly framed by thick, black lashes.

The last time she'd been this close to him was when she'd leaned over him as he'd sat behind his desk, on the pretext of checking a non-existent spot on his shirt. He'd continued talking on his phone, paying no attention to her, while she'd been thinking about the phone she'd hidden on one of the bookshelves, hoping she'd set the timer correctly and that the photos would come out okay. She been so anxious about it, she hadn't had time to even consider their proximity.

Now, though, every bit of his intense focus was on her and she had nothing else to distract her.

She'd slipped up somehow, betrayed some kind of response that had caught his attention. Stupid fool that she was. She couldn't afford mistakes, not with a man like this one.

It was only that he'd been staring at her as if he could read all her thoughts, and she'd had to protect herself somehow. She shouldn't have looked away, that was clear. Well, she wouldn't make that mistake again.

She had to remember that she hated this man. He was the direct cause of the destruction of her family, and all the years of misery after it, and she could *not* let him get under her skin simply because her idiot female hormones found him unbearably attractive.

After all, she knew where that led. Her mother had been a hopeless romantic who'd thrown everything away to follow her father, his easy charm going straight to her head, like good French champagne. Flora had been the same. She'd idolised her happy, optimistic, fun-loving father. He'd hung the moon and all the stars in the sky for her, and she loved him. And he loved her. As he'd told her so often, he would protect her. He'd never let anything bad happen to her.

But he'd lied.

He hadn't loved her at all, because if he had, he wouldn't have taken his own life, leaving her and her mother alone.

Nowadays she wasn't like her mother, a romantic fool with a head full of dreams. Love didn't sustain anyone and those dreams dissipated like smoke at one hint of reality.

The reality was a rundown flat above a chip shop, and nights alone, eating baked beans from a can, because her mother was out at her second job pulling pints in a pub, trying to earn enough money just to keep the lights on.

The reality was watching her mother slowly succumb to a slow and painful death.

Love was a lie, and she would never believe it again.

This wasn't love though, this was only physical attraction. Yet she couldn't let herself be ruled by it. She couldn't let any sign of her susceptibility to him show either. Already he saw too much, all that shattered emerald roving over her, looking for weaknesses, probing for vulnerabilities.

Bracing herself, Flora stayed where she was, blocking the delicious scent of his aftershave from her mind and ignoring the warmth of his body. She gave herself a moment to regroup, then she said, fighting to keep her voice calm. 'I don't know anything, sir. I assure you.'

This didn't seem to satisfy him as his focus only intensified, making an odd heat sweep unexpectedly through her. She could feel it in her cheeks, glowing just beneath her skin, and before she knew what she was doing, she'd pulled her chin from his grip and taken a couple of steps back, putting some distance between them.

Apollo said nothing, but his gaze had turned speculative, making her heart beat faster.

Good God, what was she thinking? Pulling away from him so suddenly was only going to make him even more curious than he already was. She'd seen that happen before, when someone interested him. He'd ask them all kinds of questions, never seeming to be bored with the answers. He might not have a charming bone in his body, but people seemed helpless to resist the concentrated beam of his attention.

She, on the other hand, was terrified of it. She'd always wondered if she'd be able to keep up her facade of smooth, capable and not at all interesting if he ever turned it on her.

Apparently not.

She smoothed her skirt and fussed with a button on her blouse, trying to hide how badly he'd flustered her.

'Perhaps it's a disgruntled employee,' she suggested, keeping her tone as even as she could. 'Or a business rival.'

He ignored the comment, his green stare sharp as knives. 'Are you afraid of me, Flora?'

This time she wasn't able to hide her shock. 'What? No, of course not.'

'Are you sure? You certainly seemed to be just now.'

Yes, she *had* given herself away. Dammit.

Her control of this situation was slowly slipping out of her grip and that couldn't happen, not when he seemed to be undermining her calm at every turn. She had to do better than this.

She and her mother had been won over by her father, time and time again, when it came to his often grandiose plans for bettering their family. Laura never seemed to learn the lesson, that David's pipe dreams were always just that. Pipe dreams. While Flora had been certain that her handsome, wonderful father would take care of them, just the way he'd promised.

Yet in the end he hadn't taken care of them at all. Apparently neither she nor her mother had been important enough to make him stay, and when he'd died, he'd left them alone. Powerless against the grief…

She would not let herself be so utterly at the mercy of another person again.

She would stay in control of her emotions and herself, and, most important of all, her plans for justice for her parents.

Ceding him even one iota of control couldn't happen, and most especially not given that he was the type of man who wouldn't just take an inch, he'd take a mile and then some.

'You startled me, that's all.' She met his gaze. 'Why on earth would I be afraid of you?'

Again, he didn't answer, merely gave her the same flat green stare. 'It would not do for you to pull away like that when we're out in public together. So, I ask again. Are you afraid of me?'

'No.' She lifted her chin and took a step towards him. 'Do you need me to prove it to you?'

Something gleamed in the depths of his eyes then, something dark and hungry, which sent a hot, electric pulse straight through her. She'd seen that gleam before, when his interest had been caught with a deal, or he'd been issued a business challenge he wanted to meet. He'd never looked at her that way though, not until now, and it stole all the breath from her lungs.

That was a mistake. You've caught the attention of a predator.

Pity there hadn't been any other options. She couldn't let him believe she was afraid of him—even though that might have been the safest course of action—she just couldn't. She wasn't anyone's helpless victim, not any more.

Still, it was too late to do anything about it now.

She *had* caught his interest, and some long-forgotten part of her, a lost, lonely part, liked that. Liked that a lot.

You can't forget what you're here for. Justice.

No, she wouldn't. But maybe there was another way to take back control of this little scenario that he'd stolen from her. A way that she'd initially discarded, because she'd thought he was passionless, and he wasn't.

You could use that interest to get close to him, and if he wants marriage, even better. As his wife you'll be able to steadily drain him dry—

No, perhaps *not* draining him dry on second thoughts. He'd said that if he fell, the company would fall too, and that company employed a lot of people. She'd ruin a lot of livelihoods if she somehow managed to financially destroy him, and her plan was only about him. She didn't want to involve anyone else or make them suffer.

Of course, she should have thought of that earlier, before she'd sent him those pictures, but she hadn't been thinking of other people at the time, only of her own cause.

How else could she see justice served?

Ruin him emotionally, the way your mother was ruined. The way your father was ruined. Break his heart, the way yours was broken...

A cold little thrill wound through her. Oh, yes, why not? She could manipulate his interest in her, potentially using that to seduce him, then make him fall in love with her and then... She'd break his heart and walk away.

A dangerous thought and terrifying, in its way. Firstly, he was an experienced man, who'd taken a variety of lovers, so seducing him might be an issue since she'd had no experience at all, which he'd definitely realise. Secondly, making him fall in love with her would be... difficult, and not least because of that little experience issue. Getting close to him would also put her own secrets at risk, so if she was going to do it, she'd have to be very, very careful indeed.

Definitely something to consider, but right now, the first thing she had to do was make sure he knew that she wasn't intimidated by him.

Inwardly bracing herself, Flora took another step, then another, coming closer to him. He didn't move. His expression was impassive, yet that gleam in his eyes continued to glitter like a fire burning deep in the jungle.

She came to a stop in front of him, her heart beating loudly in her ears as she tipped her head back to look up at him. He didn't take his gaze from hers. His arms were folded across his broad chest and, once again, getting close to him and having his delicious scent all around her made it difficult to think clearly.

'See?' She was unable to keep the faint husk from her voice. 'I'm not afraid.'

He said nothing for a long moment, merely looking down his beautifully shaped Greek nose at her, his tall, dark presence seeming to fill the generous space of the office in way it had never done before.

The moment lengthened, the air around them thickening in ways that made it feel as if all the oxygen in the room had suddenly vanished.

Then, before she could move, he reached out and cupped her cheek in one large hand. The heat of his palm was astonishing, his touch electric. Flora couldn't move, could barely even breathe.

'Does this bother you?' His voice was as cool as water on her hot skin and she had to resist the almost overwhelming desire to lean into his hand.

Her mouth was bone dry. 'No.'

'Good.' Slowly, he slid his hand along her jaw to the back of her head, cupping it gently in his palm. 'How about this?'

Her heart raced, the sound deafening her. His fingertips were pressing into her hair, that gleam in his eyes glittering brighter, sharper. 'What are you doing?' The words came out thick, but she couldn't adjust the sound of her voice.

'Testing you.' His own voice was expressionless, like stone, as if the fact that they were standing so close to each other had no effect on him whatsoever. 'We need to be comfortable touching each other if this is going to work.'

Well. Two could play at that game.

'In that case.' She lifted a hand and placed it on his chest, her fingertips resting lightly on the snowy cotton of his shirt. He felt very warm and very hard, and it was very difficult to keep hold of her usual calm, but she managed to raise a brow coolly. 'Are you comfortable with this?'

His mouth was in its usual severe line and she found herself staring at it, wondering what he would look like if it relaxed, maybe even curved.

He would be astonishing.

Oh, yes. He would be.

'Yes,' he said, his voice as steady as a rock.

Flora swallowed yet again. How was it possible to feel as if she was going to go up in flames, while he was cold as a slab of granite, and just as expressionless? It seemed desperately unfair that he should remain unaffected by her, while for her it was getting hard to think with his hand cradling the back of her head. With the heat of him seeping into her fingertips where they rested on his chest.

So unfair that she didn't really think through what she did next. The only thing that seemed important was that she had to do something to take charge of this, to exert her own power. She couldn't let him have all of it, not if she wanted justice.

So, very slowly, she curled her fingers around his tie, gripping the warm silk like a rope as she made herself hold his dark, green gaze. 'What about this?' she asked.

'Apart from the creases you're putting in my tie, yes.'

He didn't move, or betray any physical reaction to her nearness whatsoever.

It incensed her, and before she could think better of it, Flora held on to his tie, rose onto her toes, and pressed her mouth to his.

Apollo didn't like surprises, especially when it came to people's behaviour. He'd never turned his gift for reading people on Flora McIntyre before, because he'd never had to. She was there to do his bidding, and she did it. There was no need to inquire further.

So for her to grip his tie, before rising on her toes to kiss him, was the very last thing he'd expected her to do, and it shocked him so profoundly that for a long moment he couldn't move.

Then, much to his horror, everything male in him woke to full aching life, as a bolt of electricity drove all the way down his spine.

Her lips on his were light as a butterfly and so very soft, so very warm, possessing a sweet hesitancy that grabbed him by the throat and refused to let go.

He'd never felt anything like it in his entire life.

He shouldn't have pushed her about being afraid of him, he knew that, and he wasn't sure why he'd been so insistent. But then she'd lifted her chin in a way she'd never done before, and the primitive beast in him knew exactly what that meant.

A direct challenge. And the most peculiar rush of adrenaline had coursed through him. As if she'd flicked a switch in his brain, or she'd stepped out of the shadows and into the light, and he was seeing her for the first time. A woman, not merely his PA. A woman with a mind of her own, who wasn't merely a blank slate who agreed with everything he said and carried out his orders. A woman with a touch of spirit, probably more than a touch, if that chin lift was anything to go by.

He should have stopped pushing then and stepped back, returned to his usual place behind his desk, but he hadn't. That glimpse of temper had been enough to hold him where he was, to want to know more...

Yet he hadn't thought it would be this, a kiss with the kind of heat that brought a man to his knees.

He'd never denied himself physical pleasure in his quest to rebuild Helios, though his lovers were always chosen with care. Only women who wanted what he did, which was physical pleasure and nothing more.

However, when he'd decided on the next step in his plans for the Constantinides name—the engagement to Violet—he'd easily put all his lovers aside. He'd intended his marriage to Violet to be a real one, though they had not actually consummated their relationship yet. Violet had wanted to wait until their wedding night and he'd agreed. He could control himself; he wasn't desperate.

He and Violet had kissed each other of course, and it had been very pleasant, but this... Flora... This was not pleasant.

This was cataclysmic.

He found himself cupping the back of her head with both hands, his fingertips pushing into the soft thickness of her hair, holding her still as he took control of the kiss.

She shuddered, the taste of her so utterly delicious it was if he'd never tasted a woman's mouth before. Sweet and hot as melted honey, and with something more, something addictive he couldn't quite grasp, which had him shifting his grip to put the pad of his thumb on her lower lip, easing her mouth open to him so he could explore more fully.

She made a soft sound in her throat, but she wasn't pushing him away, so he didn't stop, turning the kiss hotter, deeper. Dimly something was telling him that this was a bad idea, that he'd never felt this way about her before, so why was he now? But he couldn't quite get a grasp on the answer to the question. Because why hadn't they done this before? It seemed ridiculous, when the chemistry burning between them was so hot and strong.

You're her boss, that's why. And this is for the media only. You're not supposed to actually feel this way for real.

Something ice-cold cut through the heat in his veins. That was true. So what the hell was he doing? Flora had never given him any sign she felt anything for him. She'd never flirted, never smiled, never sneaked glances at him while he wasn't looking. Never had her hand linger on his shoulder or anywhere else about his person. Of course, those pictures would seem to indicate that was a lie, but it wasn't. So why was he suddenly kissing her back? The ethical boundaries he'd placed around his business practices were there for a reason and he could not cross them. He could *not*.

With a force of will that took far more effort than it

should, Apollo wrenched his mouth from hers and let her go, taking a step back. Only to be brought up short by her small fist still wrapped around his tie.

She was holding on to it for dear life and looking up at him. Her eyes had gone dark as midnight, her cheeks stained with colour. Her mouth full and red from their kiss.

Beautiful. She's beautiful.

The thought came to him without any prompting, the urge to kiss her again was so powerful that he nearly bent his head to do just that. But he knew what happened when he gave into his darker impulses. He ruined people.

Flora had surprised him, and he couldn't allow that to happen again. Honesty was important to him, even if he was going to have to fake a marriage in order to protect her, but control was even more so. Control over his mind and his body, control over his emotions. He couldn't allow his grip to slip, not even for moment.

You're going to marry her, though. So what does it matter if you kiss her again?

He was going to marry her, it was true, but theirs would not be the kind of marriage he'd been going to enter into with Violet. That marriage had been arranged and talked about, every detail decided upon going in, with children part of the mix. An honest relationship based on what each other had wanted, no surprises. No messy emotion to complicate matters.

Which was not anything like marrying Flora. That was a spur of the moment decision, a solution to an unexpected problem, and it would only be on paper. With a quick divorce once the fuss had died down. Any physical entanglements would only make things difficult, and, apart from anything else, he was still her boss, and he had to set an example.

So, no, definitely no more kisses, or anything else of that nature.

Forcing down the heat of desire still burning in his blood, Apollo reached for her fingers gripping his tie, and gently unwrapped them from the fabric. Her skin felt warm against his, though he tried not to be conscious of it.

'I think you proved your point,' he said curtly, releasing her hand and stepping back.

Flora said nothing, her mouth still open, her eyes still dark, the colour high in her cheeks. She looked almost dazed, which gave him a disturbing amount of satisfaction. She'd never seemed anything less than serene, so for his kiss to strip that veneer of calm so completely away from her pleased him on a deep, base level.

Don't turn this into something it's not.

He wouldn't. This was an act, a show to protect Flora from any blowback, as well as for the public to keep his good name and reputation intact.

An act and that's all.

'Don't look at me like that, Flora,' he snapped. 'I'm not kissing you again, no matter how big those eyes of yours get. Do you understand?'

She flushed, a spark of bright silver glittering in her eyes. And, for a moment, he found himself holding his breath, expecting her to fling some spiky comment at him, almost hoping for it. But then the spark disappeared, and her usual serenity settled over her features.

'Yes, I understand.' She smoothed a strand of black hair that had escaped her bun behind her ear. 'So, this draft. What did you want me to include?'

It was admirable really, the way she so easily put her facade into place. Yet he couldn't seem to get that memory out of his head, of her looking up at him, eyes dark, mouth red, all dazed from that kiss. Couldn't shake, either, that very male satisfaction at how he'd ruffled that perfect calm of hers. How he'd made her grip his tie and look at him as if she was dying of thirst and he was a glass of iced water. If she was any other woman, and he a different man, it might have been interesting to play with her a little, find out if that passion he'd caught a glimpse of just before was truly—

But no. He couldn't think such things, not when he had a reputation to rescue.

'Let's go with this,' he said, turning abruptly and striding back around the side of his desk, putting some distance between them. 'You and I worked together, as you said, and our attraction was such that we couldn't fight it. You kissed me after a late-night planning session and that's when we realised we had to make a decision. I'd been going to tell Violet about us, but then the photos were released before I had the chance to do so. But now they're out in the public sphere and we're relieved that we no longer have to hide our passion.'

The colour in her cheeks was still high, the charcoal glint of her eyes still dark. '*I* kissed you?'

There was a slight edge to the question, which again had never been apparent in her voice before. In fact, she'd never questioned him before, full stop.

'Yes,' he said, frowning. 'That part is certainly true, is it not? Besides, it would be worse for my reputation if we said I kissed you first.'

'What about my reputation?' Again there was a brief glint of unfamiliar silver, her temper obviously on a short leash. 'You said you were doing this partly to protect me, don't forget.'

Interesting. She wasn't quite as adept at hiding her feelings as she'd been minutes before. Or perhaps she'd always had this sharp edge and he'd just never noticed? Maybe it was the kiss that had disturbed her…

Not that he should be thinking about that kiss. She was right, he had said he was doing this partly to protect her, and he was. The media was always harder on women, this he knew, and her reputation was as important as his.

'True,' he admitted. 'How about this then? You kissed me, but then you were extremely apologetic and offered to resign. I, naturally, wouldn't hear of it.'

Her gaze narrowed, but she nodded. 'Okay. But we haven't touched each other beyond those photos. We wanted to go public before anything more happened between us.'

Excellent. She wanted to put that kiss behind them too, which was definitely where it should be.

'Agreed,' he said. 'Our relationship has not been con-summated. You insisted on waiting until we were married.'

Once again, faint colour touched her cheekbones. 'Do we really need to say that?'

'No, but it's better if we have an answer if the question is asked. And someone will, because the general public is inordinately interested in people's sex lives. Those photos being a prime example.'

'Very well.' Her facade was back in place again.

'Good.' He dug his phone out of his pocket and glanced down at it, scrolling through his calendar. They'd need to be seen together as quickly as possible, and preferably at some major event. 'Tomorrow night I have that gala in Paris. That will be the perfect time to debut our relationship.'

'Tomorrow night?' The edge had returned to Flora's voice, surprise flickering through her dark grey eyes.

Strange that she hadn't thought this through. Normally she was excellent at anticipating and then coping with any difficulties. Then again, perhaps it was because she was personally involved this time. Also, that kiss...

Irritation coiled inside him as the warmth of her mouth on his lingered in his brain. He shoved it away with more firmness this time.

'Yes, tomorrow night. You know how fast and how far gossip travels. We need to release a public statement as quickly as possible, then follow it up with a public appearance together, as a couple.'

This time there was only the slightest flicker of a reaction, before her expression smoothed once more. Whatever control she'd lost, she now had it back in her grasp.

Too late, though. You know who she is now. Who she really is.

Yes, he did, and he would do precisely nothing about it. Regardless of what act they'd put on for the public, he wouldn't touch her. He was still her boss, and doing anything with her at all would be crossing one of the many lines he'd drawn in his quest to rehabilitate the Constantinides name.

Not to mention rehabilitating yourself, too.

Yes, that also.

'Fine,' Flora said expressionlessly. 'Paris it is.'

Apollo put his phone away and sat down at his desk. 'The situation is in hand then. Get working on that draft. I want it on my desk in an hour.'

CHAPTER FOUR

THE NEXT EVENING Flora found herself standing in front of a full-length mirror in the bedroom of the eighteenth-century Constantinides mansion in Paris's Marais district.

They'd arrived from London a couple of hours earlier. Apollo upsetting Flora's usual organisational routine whenever they arrived anywhere by ordering her to stop fussing, that Madame Choubert, the housekeeper, would be taking over her duties for the remainder of the visit.

She hadn't known what to do then, but a minute after that an officious French designer arrived with a rack full of gowns and Flora was hustled into the bedroom to try them all on, in a quest to find something suitable for the event that evening.

Flora tried to tell Apollo that she'd brought one of the plain black gowns that she customarily wore when she accompanied him to events as his PA, but he flatly refused to even look at it. It wasn't suitable, he told her shortly. She needed to wear something more befitting her new role as his fiancée.

He was right, of course, but as the hour of the event

drew closer, all her insides were tying themselves in knots, her palms sweaty.

She only just managed to stop herself from wiping them on the gown's midnight-blue silk as she stared at herself in the mirror. The gown had small cap sleeves, and a fitted bodice, but the drama came from the skirt, all swathed and gathered on one side at her hip, leaving her pretty stilettos in the same midnight-blue on display, with the rest of it falling away into a dramatic train behind her.

It really was the most beautiful gown. Discreetly sexy, showing a flash of one thigh where the fabric gathered, and highlighting her bare shoulders, neck and cleavage.

She didn't recognise herself wearing it. She looked like a different person. Not the hardworking, colourless PA, who'd dedicated her life to taking her boss's orders and resolutely staying in the background, but a glamorous, beautiful woman, fully worthy of the title of Apollo Constantinides's fiancée.

But you're not worthy. You're lying to him.

Flora ignored the thought as the designer paced around her, twitching fabric here and there, and murmuring *'magnifique'* at intervals.

Yes, she absolutely was lying to him, but she didn't care. He hadn't cared when he'd talked her father into investing every cent of her family's savings into that awful scheme, so why should she?

In fact, now she thought about it, she could see where her mother was coming from when she'd refused to accept Apollo's compensation money. Blood money, Laura had called it, and at the time, Flora hadn't understood her refusal since they'd needed it.

Now, as an adult, she understood. No amount of money could ever make up for the loss of a husband and father, so what did a few little lies matter?

They didn't. Just like Apollo didn't. And so, she was going to break his heart the way hers and her mother's had been broken, and she wouldn't feel any regret, not a shred.

That will never bring your father or your mother back, you know this.

It wouldn't, but she hadn't spent the last few years of her life working to get close enough to him to put her plans in motion to stop now, not over one little lie.

She'd only be satisfied once he'd felt the same grief and pain she had.

Anyway, she couldn't start second-guessing herself, especially not when she was going to be the centre of attention tonight. She had to be brave, not let the nerves get to her, no matter that she was more used to staying out of the spotlight rather than standing in its centre.

That morning had already been chaotic, with the photos hitting the media overnight, and now global news platforms were full of sensational headlines complete with those grainy shots she'd leaked. Apollo had approved the press release she'd drafted, which had then gone to Violet for approval also, before being sent out to various media organisations in response.

Violet's people had put out a press release of their own, and it had been measured and gracious, with a little white lie detailing how Apollo had been to see her personally and how they'd worked things out. She wished him all the best with his engagement.

Really, Flora couldn't fault Apollo's handling of the situation. He'd controlled things masterfully. He wouldn't allow a dignified silence where other rumours could take root and grow, ordering all requests for interviews to go directly to him. He refused none of them, answering every question with his usual blunt honesty, as well as very real regret, admitting to his love affair with Flora, and acknowledging that this was a bad look given his stance on employer/employee relations and general business ethics.

He did not charm. He did not manipulate. And, as per usual, people liked it, they found it refreshing in a world full of spin, and she just knew he was going to get the entire world on his side again. And as for her...

Flora swallowed, staring sightlessly at herself in the mirror as the nerves returned.

She'd woken that morning to hundreds of text messages and voicemails from the media, all asking for interviews. Which she'd expected. But she'd also hoped that most of the attention would be directed towards Apollo rather than her.

However, given the spin the Helios PR department was putting on the situation—that she was supposedly the love of Apollo's life—she was every bit an object of interest as he was.

Tonight would be difficult, she was under no illusion.

Because tonight everyone's eyes would be on her, studying her, whispering about her, wondering about her.

Tonight might be the start of all her secrets being uncovered.

The few flimsy smokescreens she'd put in place to hide her family history hadn't been designed to withstand concentrated scrutiny by journalists, or the internet at large, and it wouldn't take a lot of research to discover that McIntyre was her mother's maiden name. That her real name was Florence, not Flora. That she was the daughter of David Hunt, one of Stavros Constantinides's victims, who'd killed himself after hearing rumours that the Constantinides scheme was a Ponzi scheme, prompting the police to investigate Helios.

She couldn't risk that happening, not when her quest for justice had only just started.

You're an idiot. Another thing you should have anticipated.

She hadn't though. She hadn't anticipated that Apollo would take her ruination plan and turn it into a triumph, while leaving her at the mercy of the press. Oh, he'd said he'd protect her, but how could he, when he didn't know the secrets she was hiding from him?

She moistened her dry mouth, a headache starting to throb behind her eyes, which she ignored as she glanced at Apollo, standing by the windows.

He wasn't looking at her, his attention was on his phone. He'd wanted to approve the gown, and so far had vetoed all the ones she'd tried on. She didn't know what exactly he wanted, but he hadn't said yes to anything yet.

Light from the setting sun shone through the windows of the bedroom, glossing his black hair and limning his profile in gold. He was already dressed for the evening, all in black, the perfect contrast to his olive skin.

Tall, dark and dangerous.

God, he really was the most outrageously handsome man.

She resented it. Or, more specifically, she resented the way everything female in her was aware of everything male in him, on the most basic level.

It had been that kiss, that was the trouble. That kiss and her reaction to it.

She'd thought she'd be able to kiss him and feel nothing, to use that glint of hunger she'd seen in his eyes to her own advantage. Perhaps unsettle him as badly as he'd unsettled her, and yet, the moment her lips had touched his, she'd been lost.

Heat had consumed her, a hunger rising inside her that she didn't understand. She'd been powerless against it, and then, when he'd started kissing her back, she'd forgotten everything. She'd forgotten that she hated him. Forgotten all her plans for his ruin. Forgotten that her identity was a secret and he could never find out.

Forgotten her own name.

All there had been was the heat of his mouth and the taste of him, wild and dark and raw. The feeling of his fingers pressing into her hair, the heat of his body, and his scent that stole all the breath from her lungs.

It had been a long time since anyone had touched her, not since her mother had held on to her hand the day she'd died in hospital years earlier, and Flora hadn't known how starved she was for someone's touch until Apollo had threaded his fingers into her hair.

She'd wanted his arms around her. She'd wanted his hands on her, stroking her, caressing her. She wanted more than one kiss. And when he'd lifted his head and looked down into her eyes, all she could think was, *Again, please. Kiss me again.*

But he hadn't. And, worse, he'd seen the desire she hadn't been able to hide. He knew exactly how hungry she was for him physically.

She hated herself for it, but there was nothing to be done. She couldn't take it back now.

As if he'd felt her gaze on him, Apollo looked up from his phone suddenly, and their eyes met, and for a second it was like that moment back in his office, after she'd kissed him, the air around them thick with sexual tension.

Then his eyes widened slightly as he took in the gown, and the breath rushed out of her as that dark, predator's gleam caught in his gaze.

He liked the gown, it was obvious.

Unexpected heat washed through her, and while it made the nerves fluttering around inside her worse, it also gave her a measure of reassurance.

Yes, she could do this seduction thing. He'd seemed so unaffected by that kiss, yet was that really true? He'd been very firm when he'd told that there would be no more kisses, but she could change his mind. She would have to. Her revised quest for justice depended on it, after all.

The designer said something in French to Apollo, then disappeared through the door, shutting it firmly behind him.

Flora took a steadying, silent breath as Apollo strode to where she stood, then walked a slow circle around her, scanning her from every angle.

'Yes,' he murmured to himself, his voice a low rumble. 'This is the one. Jacques has really outdone himself this time.'

Flora tried to resist the blush that crept into her cheeks, but there was no stopping it as he lifted his dark green gaze to hers. 'This is much better than the gown you brought,' he said. 'The press will not be disappointed either.'

He sounded cool, yet the look in his eyes was anything but. She wanted desperately to rip her gaze from his, but being coy wasn't going to help her plan, so she ignored the butterflies and stared back at him instead. 'I hope so,' she said, wishing she sounded as cool as he did, not sick with nerves.

'You'll be fine.' He gazed at her a moment longer, then put his hand in his pocket, pulling out a black velvet box. 'I want you to wear this.' Flipping open the lid, he held it out to her.

Flora's heart beat faster, though she had no idea why. It was an engagement ring, and of course it was an engagement ring. She was supposed to be his fiancée, and fiancées generally wore rings.

The ring comprised a single large blue diamond on a platinum band, bright and costly looking as it glittered against the black velvet.

Flora stared at it, the tension inside her pulling tighter and tighter. It wasn't the same as the ring he'd given Violet, and she should know, since she'd organised the purchase of it. He'd chosen it, though, and had spent a good deal of time over the choice, eventually settling on an emerald the same colour as his eyes.

Had he spent time choosing this one? Had it mattered to him which one he bought? Or had he ordered someone to purchase it for him?

But no, thinking about the stupid ring was ridiculous. Of course it hadn't mattered to him, none of this did. The ring was for show, just like the gown, and her attendance at the gala this evening. None of it was real, not even a little bit.

'Please tell me you didn't spend a lot on this,' she said, trying to cover her nerves.

He lifted a shoulder in an elegant shrug. 'I spent enough for it to look like an engagement ring. People will be noting it, so it wouldn't do for it to look like I spent nothing.' When she didn't move, still staring at it, he made an impatient sound and took the ring out, discarding the box on a small side table nearby. 'Here,' he said peremptorily. 'Give me your hand.'

She didn't want to. She didn't want him to touch her, especially given how badly she'd betrayed herself with that kiss the day before. Then again, refusing him now would betray something else, and she couldn't do that either.

Steeling herself, Flora extended her hand and tried to ignore the inevitable pulse of electricity that bolted through her as he took her fingers in his. He remained impassive as he pushed the ring onto her finger, then held her hand a moment, looking down at the ring glittering there.

His fingers were warm, his grip firm. She could feel her skin tightening in response, her breath getting short.

No, this was madness. She couldn't allow him to get to her like this. What she wanted was for him to be affected by her, not the other way around. She hated him. She *couldn't* want him, she just couldn't. He'd ruined her family, destroyed them completely, and she should not be getting breathless just because he was holding her hand.

He looked up, his green gaze capturing hers. 'Do you like it?'

'Like what?' God, she sounded like a teenage girl with her first crush. 'Oh, the ring? Yes. It's very pretty.'

Unexpectedly, he enclosed her hand in his, the warmth of his palm surrounding her, and it was such a shock that she couldn't move. Every part of her seemed to zero in on his large hand holding hers. Long, blunt fingers, his knuckles dotted with a few white long-healed scars. A strong, masculine hand.

No one had ever held her hand the way he was doing so now. Oh, maybe long ago, in the mists of childhood, her parents might have, but not that she remembered.

Since her mother had died, all there'd been in her life was rigid determination. She'd allowed herself nothing that wasn't in pursuit of her goal—to get as close as she could to Apollo Constantinides. Now, she *was* close and, in a way she'd never imagined, all she could think about was how good it was to feel someone's hand gripping hers. As if there was not only warmth there, but support too.

Apollo frowned slightly. 'Your fingertips are cold. Are you nervous?'

Briefly, she debated lying to him, but he was looking intently at her now, his focus narrow and sharp, and she knew she couldn't. He'd realise, which would then prompt more questions, and she couldn't face that, not now. So all she said was, 'Maybe a little.'

Strangely, his gaze softened just a bit, as if it mattered to him that she was nervous. 'Don't be,' he said, his voice shaded with an edge of something unfamiliar. 'Yes, the press will likely be in our faces all night, but I'll keep you from the worst of them, understand?'

Another little shock of surprise rippled through her. In the year she'd spent working for him, all she'd seen of him was the cold, ruthless businessman, who was blunt to the point of offensiveness. She'd never seen him be reassuring, not to anyone.

She'd never seen the faint concern in his eyes as he looked at her, or felt the warmth of his grip. She'd never experienced the strange rush of relief that accompanied it either, as if a part of her wanted to believe that, yes, he would protect her.

It had been a very long time since anyone had cared

for her or worried for her. Since her mother had died, she'd thrown herself into her quest for justice, and because she'd had to hide her background, she'd allowed no one to get too close.

Bizarrely, the person she spent the most time with was the man standing in front of her now. The man she hated, who was holding her hand, giving her reassurance.

The man you'll be betraying.

Flora pulled her hand from his abruptly, the warmth of his touch lingering on her skin. 'Thank you,' she said quickly, hoping he wouldn't notice how sharp the movement had been. 'As you said, I'm sure I'll be fine.'

Flora was not fine. Apollo was certain of it.

He'd been momentarily robbed of speech just before, as he'd looked up from his phone and seen her standing there, all those delicious feminine curves wrapped in midnight-blue silk. He was so used to her in her PA uniform of white shirt, black skirt and plain black pumps, it had never occurred to him how she might look in a ballgown.

Well, now he had the answer. She looked beautiful. Glorious. Stunning.

He was noticing all kinds of other things about her too, aspects he couldn't remember seeing before. Such as how the deep charcoal of her eyes reminded him of grey diamonds, silvery and dark at the same time. Her full mouth and its gentle pout. The tender skin of her throat, the pale vulnerability of her bare shoulders. The glossy fall of her curly black hair.

They were all physical things, and he shouldn't be noticing them, yet somehow that switch she'd flipped in him the day before was resolutely set to 'on', and he couldn't seem to ignore it.

Perhaps it was merely that for the past three months he'd been celibate and it was wearing on him. He had, after all, been waiting for his wedding night with Violet, and that was now no longer going to happen.

Perhaps you could have one with Flora...

The thought wound through his head, prompting an immediate physical response, though he crushed it before it could fully take hold.

No, he would not be having anything with Flora. He would not cross that line. He was supposed to be protecting her, not taking advantage of her. Yes, after tonight, the world would think that they were already sleeping together, so it wouldn't be as if he was risking anything publicly. But *he* would know.

He'd crossed lines before thinking they didn't matter, and the end result had been a man's death. He wasn't going to do it again. Some of the press might call him rigid, inflexible and lacking in empathy, but he didn't care. His supposed lack of empathy was simply him being too blunt and too honest, and he wasn't going to apologise for that. He wasn't like his father, full of smiles and empty charm. Oh, once he had been. Once he'd been as well known for it as his father had. He'd enjoyed it too, using that charm and his good looks to get people on his side, manipulating them with ease. That had always given him such an adrenaline rush.

But that had been then, before David Hunt had killed himself.

Apollo had been twenty when that happened, which had been far too young for such a harsh lesson. He'd learned it just the same, though. The recklessness that his father had was in him too. They were both gamblers, enjoying the rush and the thrill when the bets paid off, giving no heed to the consequences.

He had to guard against it, not let anything go to his head, and the problem with Flora was that she did. She was a slippery slope, and he couldn't risk falling down it.

This would merely be a business arrangement between them, nothing more.

Violet had been very gracious about the photos, and he'd even suggested that perhaps, after an appropriate interval of time had passed, they could resume their engagement. She hadn't refused, so maybe the option was still available.

The reaction of the media to the photos had been predictable, but he wasn't concerned. Not now that Flora had agreed to their little sham affair.

What he was concerned about was the pale look on Flora's face and that, when he'd held her hand, her fingertips had been cold. He'd wanted to keep holding that hand, keep it enclosed in his to warm her, but then she'd pulled it away, and quite abruptly.

He studied her, noting the faint wash of colour on

her cheeks and the way she was fussily smoothing her skirt, thick dark lashes veiling her gaze. The diamond on the ring he'd bought the night before glittered on her finger. A blue diamond, because it was the biggest and most expensive ring he could get on such short notice. It suited her.

That flush in her cheeks suited her too. Was that him? Because he'd touched her? It was, he was sure. Especially given her reaction to the kiss the day before.

Not that you'll be doing anything about it.

Of course he wouldn't, but still… Had she always felt that way about him? Or was this a new attraction she'd suddenly discovered, ignited by that kiss?

Whatever, they weren't questions he was going to get answers to, so why he kept thinking about them was anyone's guess. What he should be thinking about was the gala they were attending tonight, and how she was going to cope with it. He was used to the public eye, but Flora wasn't. Normally she was his adjunct, not the centre of attention, so this would be a new experience for her.

'You are not fine,' he said. 'And if you pull away from me tonight the way you did just then, you will cause unwanted gossip that we both can ill afford.'

Her gaze flickered. 'I'm sorry,' she said stiffly. 'That wasn't my intention.'

'I know it wasn't.' He frowned, searching her face. 'Just what about this evening is upsetting you? Is it the attention? Because I already told you, I'll protect you from that.'

She gave him a smile that looked so forced it was as

if she'd cut it out of a magazine and pasted it on. 'Perhaps I'm…a little concerned, but I'm sure I'll be fine.'

She was lying. He could always tell a lie. But there wasn't much point in pushing her now. They didn't have long before they needed to leave.

'In that case.' He held out his hand once more. 'Come, we should practice a few poses, so we look as relaxed and as natural as possible with each other.'

It was very subtle, but he saw the instant she stiffened, as if she was bracing herself for a blow. This *was* upsetting for her, he could see the apprehension in her eyes.

Apollo had never been a man who offered comfort to people, or at least not after he and his father had ruined people's lives. Elena had blamed him for the ruination of their family, too, even though it had been his father who'd conceived and carried out the entire scheme. Apollo couldn't argue with her, not when he'd been complicit. But after Stavros had gone to jail, his mother had refused all Apollo's offers of comfort and reassurance. She'd carried her pain and anger alone, even after Stavros had died, and sometimes Apollo wondered if she'd held on to it simply so that she could throw it in his face. He was, after all, the reason his father had gone to jail.

However, it was clear that Flora needed more than brusquely worded orders. Throwing her into the deep end of the shark-infested waters of the world's press, and expecting her to swim, wasn't exactly kind, especially when none of this had been her fault.

'Flora,' he said, softening his voice. 'It will be all right. I've already told you that I won't allow your reputation to suffer and I won't. I won't permit the press to be rude to you, either, I promise.'

She stared at him for a moment, and he was sure he saw surprise cross her face. Then she reached for his hand and he took it, drawing her closer. 'That's it,' he murmured, staring down into her eyes. 'Keep looking at me like that.'

Colour had risen once again beneath her skin, the soft rose making her eyes glimmer, the grey river stones revealing chips of mica that sparkled, catching the light.

She really was very pretty.

The flush in her cheeks crept down her neck and he could track its path, the midnight-blue silk of her neckline leaving her shoulders bare, offering a tantalising glimpse of the shadow between her full breasts.

'I was wrong,' he heard himself say. 'You are not just suitable, Flora. You are exquisite.'

Should you really have said that?

Her eyes widened. 'Sir... I...'

Oh, he shouldn't have said it, he definitely shouldn't. But it was too late to take it back. He had to commit to it now.

'Not sir,' he said. 'Not tonight. Tonight, you will have to get used to calling me Apollo. And yes, you should absolutely keep blushing like that.'

He thought she might look away then, but she didn't. She kept on looking up at him, even as he put one hand on her silken hip and brought her nearer, so her body was drawn gently against his. As if they were dancing or merely being close to each other. Enjoying each other's company. Desperately in love...

She felt soft and very warm, and for some reason he couldn't remember the last time a woman had stood this close to him. Ridiculous, when it was probably Violet, and not too long ago either, but still, he couldn't recall the moment. All he could think about was Flora pressed against him, and he hadn't known until now what a revelation that would be. Because that's what she was. A revelation.

The silvery grey glitter of her eyes seemed to brighten as she lifted her hands the way she had the day before and laid them both on his chest. She only pressed lightly, and yet it was as if he could feel every whorl and twist of her fingerprints through the cotton of his shirt. As if he was a lock, keyed to her, and all he needed was her touch to open.

This is madness. What are you doing?

It *was* madness, and yet he made no move to pull away. Because the dark, devious part of his mind, the manipulative part that had led all those investors to their ruin, was already ticking over, noting her response to him, how the chemistry between them was excellent, thinking of ways to make it even more pronounced, so that no one would doubt the story he'd concocted. Wanting to feel once again the rush of seeing people dance to his tune…

He should stop. He should let her go and move away.

But his hand on her hip tightened, the other lifting slowly to cradle her cheek, the way he had the day before, the softness of her skin against his palm. And somehow his heart missed a beat as she leaned into it, looking up at him from beneath thick, black lashes.

How had he never seen her loveliness? How had he missed the tension in the air between them, which he was sure hadn't been there before? Had he been blind? Or maybe he'd deliberately not seen it, because he'd known what a temptation she'd be?

'I'm sorry I kissed you yesterday,' she said unexpectedly, a slight husk in her voice. 'I crossed a line, and I shouldn't have. I should have apologised then, but I… didn't.'

For a second his brain was so fogged trying to discern what delicious perfume she was wearing that he didn't understand what she was saying.

Then he did, and yet it still didn't make any sense. Apologise for that astonishing kiss? Was she mad?

Your sexual harassment policy? That you were very firm about afterwards? Remember that?

Yes. God. And that should be front and centre in his mind right now. So why was he thinking about her perfume and the softness of her body against his? Why was he thinking about the colour of her eyes?

This was madness and taking it any further was wrong. He'd always thought his control was perfect, but maybe it wasn't as perfect as he'd assumed it to be.

Or maybe it's because it's Flora.

No, he couldn't countenance that. She was his PA. They were going to enter into a sham relationship and marriage, but the operative word was 'sham'. It wouldn't be real. None of this was.

You're really going to endure six months of celibacy for the sake of a sham marriage?

He didn't want to, no, but what other choice was there? He couldn't risk an affair with anyone else, not after those photos had come to light. He had to be on his best behaviour and usually that wasn't a problem, so why it was hard now—in all sense of the word— he had no idea.

'It's all right,' he said coolly. 'I understood that you were trying to prove a point. Now…' With as much calm as he could muster, he took his hand away from her cheek, and released her hip before stepping back. 'Are you ready for our public debut?'

Her hands fluttered a little as he moved away, as if now they weren't resting on his chest she didn't know quite what to do with them. But her expression held its customary impassiveness, the apprehension that had been in her eyes gone.

'Yes,' she said calmly. 'I am. Apollo.'

CHAPTER FIVE

FLORA'S HEART WAS beating so loud and so fast she wondered if she might faint.

The event was being held in a lavish, eighteenth-century palace that had been lit up like Versailles, with lights that mimicked flickering candles. At the front was a set of magnificent sweeping stairs, where the paparazzi had gathered like flies, taking photographs of the rich and famous as they made their way inside.

The gala was for a well-known children's charity and Helios was a major donor, hence Apollo's invite. Normally, Flora would have leaped from the limo first before rushing around, managing his timetable for the evening, checking guest lists and making sure the people he wanted to speak to were available, not to mention also ensuring that the people who wanted to speak to him did so.

But now it was different. Now, she was on his arm, and there was nothing to manage but her own reckless hormones, which was turning out to be far more difficult than she'd ever imagined.

Back in the Constantinides residence, before they'd

left, he'd taken her in his arms and she'd been powerless to move. Powerless to resist. He'd drawn her close, one large hand pressed to her hip, the other cupping her cheek, and she hadn't been able to think.

He'd been so gentle with her, that was the trouble, and it was something she hadn't expected. That such a cold, blunt man could ever have such gentleness inside him had been a surprise, let alone him turning it on her.

He would never let the press hurt her, that's what he'd promised, and some part of her very much wanted to believe that. Some part of her very much wanted his protection, and that was insanity. She'd believed her father when he'd told her he'd always look after her, and look how that had ended.

Apart from anything else, he was also the man who'd caused her father's downfall, so how could she want that from him? He could she want him, full stop?

She didn't understand, but not knowing didn't change the fact that she did, in fact, want him, no matter how much her mind told her that it was wrong.

Not that she had much time to think about it, because Apollo had now got out of the limo and was in the process of opening the door for her, letting in a sudden cacophony from outside, people shouting and calling and clapping.

Now was the moment of truth. Now she had to get out of the car and present herself to the world as Apollo's fiancée. Now she had to pretend that she was desperately in love with him, and had crossed all kinds of boundaries to be with him.

Now she had to ignore the fact that this entire situation was of her own making and that if she had anyone to blame for it, it was herself.

Gripping hard to her courage, Flora had no choice but to step out of the limo.

Instantly they were mobbed by paparazzi, all calling out to her and using her name, as if they knew her. She felt momentarily bewildered by the scrum, not knowing where to look or how to respond. Then Apollo's hand came to rest gently at the small of her back, the warmth of his powerful figure beside her as he urged her up the stairs.

'Ignore them,' he murmured in her ear, his breath warming her skin. 'We'll walk to the top of the stairs and then pause to give them a photo op. Relax and follow my lead.'

So she did, allowing the pressure of that warm hand resting at the base of her spine to guide her as she climbed the stairs, hoping desperately that she wouldn't fall flat on her face. It had all seemed so much easier when the attention wasn't on her, when she was merely managing the situation rather than taking part.

At the top of the stairs, she turned around when Apollo did. and when he slid an arm around her waist as the cameras flashed, she let herself rest against his side so the press could get their photos.

She was very conscious of the questions people were shouting at Apollo, such as how did he reconcile his business practices with an affair with his PA? Had they slept together? What did Violet think? Was he worried that he might lose some major investors? Et cetera, et cetera. Then there were the questions shouted at her, such as who made the first move? Was she still his PA? Did she have any comment about the rumours that Violet had stormed into the Helios offices demanding an explanation?

'Ignore those questions too,' Apollo said quietly, somehow making himself heard beneath the cacophony. 'Flash the ring and smile.'

So she did, the smile feeling forced and fake.

'Yes,' Apollo said, answering one shouted question. 'Flora is my fiancée, and we'll be getting married as soon as we can. And yes, Violet has given us her blessing. If you have any more questions, please direct them to my PR people.'

Then, without saying anything further, he turned around and stalked inside the building, ushering her along with him.

Inside it was less chaotic, with music from a string quartet playing, the interior of the old ballroom lit by glittering chandeliers, with bouquets of white roses overflowing from urns and vases and large copper buckets. Wait staff circulated, carrying trays of various drinks and small canapés.

Apollo snagged them both a couple of tall flutes of champagne before finding a quiet part of the ballroom near some stairs.

She was breathing fast, her adrenaline spiking, making her feel as if she'd just taken a trip on a wild and terrifying rollercoaster.

'You did well on the stairs with the paparazzi,' Apollo

said, his attention on the crowd in the ballroom. 'Now we have to be convincing for everyone else.'

Flora took a steadying sip of champagne, the dry yeasty flavour exploding deliciously on her tongue. Now she was here, and the initial chaos of the photographers was over and done with, she felt better.

It was fine, she could do this. Her hormones might be all over the place when it came to Apollo, but all she actually had to do was trust in them. She didn't have to hide her attraction to him here. In fact, hiding it was what she *shouldn't* do.

She just had to remember that her very real feelings were supposed to be an act.

You also have to remember that the potential for all your secrets to come tumbling out has never been higher.

The shard of ice that had lodged inside her the day before, when Apollo had told her how he'd solve the issue of the photos, seemed to gain sharp edges.

It wouldn't take much interest from the media to blow her fragile cover, and given the scrum on the way in, the media *would* want to know. They'd want to know who she was and where she'd come from. What exactly was it about her that was enough to tempt a man such as Apollo Constantinides. A man famous for his spotless, impeccable reputation.

But now she was caught between a rock and a hard place, with no choice but to keep going.

She had to hope any discovery the press made about her real identity wouldn't be until *after* she'd gone through with her heartbreak plans. And if it was before? Well, she'd cross that bridge when she came to it. Right now, she had to get through this night.

'Thank you,' she said, a warm glow expanding in her chest in response to his praise, which was silly of her. Then again, he wasn't a man who gave out praise often. For example the most he'd ever given her was 'adequate'.

Wrong. He also called you exquisite, remember?

The warm glow grew warmer at the memory. She'd never even been called pretty before, let alone exquisite, and even though she might tell herself it didn't matter, that she didn't care what he thought of her, a part of her had loved that he'd said it. He wasn't a man who dispensed compliments, so it meant something coming from him.

Stop thinking about this. You can't let him distract you from what you're supposed to be doing.

No, she couldn't. She had to keep her eye on the prize, remember what she was here for, which was to get close to him. Make herself irresistible to him, make him love her. Then break that cold heart of his before anyone found out the truth about her.

Justice must be served.

Justice for her father, for her mother, and for herself.

'Are you ready to brave the rest of the room?' Apollo asked. 'You can let me do the talking if you'd prefer.'

The champagne must have loosened her tongue, because she found herself smiling up at him, and saying, 'Really? With your famous people skills? You hate doing the talking.'

His jungle green gaze settled on her, focusing with

the laser intent that indicated she'd said something that
had surprised him.

A dark little thrill arrowed through her. Good. That
meant she had to keep on surprising him, make sure he
forgot all about Flora the PA, who never teased or flirted
or disagreed with him in any way. She had to become
Flora, his fiancée. The femme fatale who was exquisite
and surprising, intriguing and passionate.

A liar...

Flora shoved that thought away hard.

'I'll manage.' His tone was brusque, but the look in
his eyes glittered.

Well, the die was cast. She had to commit to her new
plan and she had to do it now, when they were on display, even though her experience with seduction was nil.

She was just going to have to wing it.

Taking a risk, Flora stepped closer to him, looking up
at him from beneath her lashes. 'I'll be okay, Apollo,'
she said, relishing saying his name. 'Thank you for being
concerned about me, though.'

He didn't look away. 'Give me your hand,' he ordered
softly.

'You have a thing for hands, don't you?' She extended
it, feeling the usual jolt as he took hold of it.

'Just yours.' He raised her hand to his mouth and
pressed the lightest of kisses on the back of it, his hunt-
er's gaze locked on hers.

Another thrill shot through her at the heat of his lips
on her skin, her heart beating even faster.

'I assume that was for the press?' She didn't bother to hide the breathlessness in her voice.

'Of course.' One black brow rose. 'Did you want it to be for you?'

She should say no, of course she didn't want it to be for herself. This was an act, a show. This was pretend. Except what came out of her mouth was, 'Maybe.' And then she added, 'Pull me in closer.'

Something flared in his eyes then, a flame, and abruptly she found it difficult to breathe. He obviously liked this side of her, because he didn't hesitate, tugging her towards him, bringing her so close they were almost touching. She breathed him in, relaxing her tense muscles, because it didn't matter if she allowed herself to revel in his presence, to let her desire show in her eyes. This was all part of her plan.

Then she lifted a hand to his hair, touching the thick, inky softness, brushing a strand back from his brow. A tender touch that a woman might give to the man she loved.

His eyes widened as she touched him, which meant once again she'd surprised him, and that flame lost deep in the jungle green burned higher, brighter.

Flora couldn't look away.

Then he reached out slowly, almost lazily, and slid his fingers into her hair, tilting her head back, before capturing her mouth with his.

Apollo hadn't intended to kiss her. In fact, it was something he'd told himself he absolutely wasn't going to do.

All that was needed was for them to stand close to each other, for his arm to go around her waist in a decorous embrace, that was all the touching required.

Except then he'd taken her hand and kissed the back of it, and then she'd touched his hair in a natural, familiar way, and he hadn't been able to stop himself from taking things further and tasting her mouth. Even now, with her lips warm and silky beneath his, he didn't fully understand how he'd got to this point.

Perhaps it had been the way she'd touched him just before, gently, hesitantly, as if he was a work of art and she was afraid of breaking him. No one had ever touched him like that, not even when he'd been a child, and it had robbed him of breath. The silvery glints of mica in her grey eyes had been glittering, and her mouth had had the most delectable curve. He hadn't seen her smile, he'd realised with a small, electric jolt, not even once, and that was clearly a tragedy. Because her smile was a thing of beauty, and he found himself thinking of all the things he could do to get her to smile at him that way again.

It was madness.

Madness to draw her in as she'd suggested. Madness to have her so close, the sweet scent of her surrounding him and making his mouth water. Making him remember that kiss, and how delicious she had tasted.

Madness to kiss her again, especially when he knew how addicted he was to the rush and adrenaline surge that came with doing something reckless.

Yet he just couldn't stop.

He could blame it on the media, that it was part of

their performance tonight to convince everyone that they were actually in love, but deep down he knew the truth.

He wanted to kiss her to see if the chemistry that had lit him up inside the day before was still hot, still strong, and yes. It was. It very definitely was.

Yet again, there was glory in her lips against his, silky and soft. She tasted of champagne and strawberries, the kind of summers that contained picnics and ice cream and swimming in the sea under the hot sun. The kind of summers he'd only ever had as a child back in Athens, back when his father was still the hero Apollo had looked up to, not the charlatan he'd turned out to be.

Summers where his mother had loved him and not blamed him for the ruination of their family.

Summers he would never have again.

His fingers tightened in Flora's hair, curling into a fist, holding her tightly as he chased that sweet summer taste, his tongue pushing into her mouth, exploring deeper.

She made a husky, needy sound deep in her throat and leaned into him, her body pressing to his, all heat and softness. There was a hunger to her that he found almost unbearably sexy, because it had been an age since anyone had been this hungry for him. Violet certainly hadn't been. She'd enjoyed his kisses, but he knew she'd been as ambivalent as he was about the thought of actually sleeping together.

Flora wasn't ambivalent. Her blatant desire for him was the purest aphrodisiac he'd ever known, and he wanted to crush her to him, tear the midnight-blue silk from her shoulders and explore the silken curves of her body. Stroke them. Taste them. Bury himself inside them…

But he couldn't. Not here, and not anywhere else either.

She was untouchable. She was on the other side of all the boundaries he'd put around himself, and he couldn't cross over them. He wouldn't. That way lay the slippery slope into ruination, and he'd already been there once before. Someone had died because of him, because he'd grown addicted to the rush, the surge of adrenaline that had hit him whenever he'd talked another person into investing in his father's scheme.

But he'd liked the admiration and approval in Stavros's eyes even more.

Love had led him down that slope, and he couldn't even set foot on it, which meant he had to be on his guard.

With as much gentleness as he could muster, Apollo relaxed his grip on her hair and lifted his mouth from hers. She was delicately flushed, her grey eyes glowing with desire, and he knew it was for him. It was *all* for him. His beautiful PA, and yes, she *was* beautiful. He'd been right about what he'd said to her earlier that day. She wasn't just beautiful, she was exquisite.

His heart was a drum in his ears and there was a tightness in his groin that definitely shouldn't be there. Damn. What had he been thinking? He had to be better than this.

'Come,' he said brusquely, releasing her. 'There are people I need to introduce you to.'

He couldn't bear it suddenly, to keep on looking at her

lovely face and the desire in her eyes, so he turned to the rest of the room and took a step towards the crowd. Only to be brought up short as she grabbed his hand, her fingers lacing through his, as if he belonged to her and she was staking her claim.

Strange to be the one who suddenly wanted to pull away. To be the one putting distance between them. Given her earlier responses, he'd expected it to be her, not him, who couldn't bear their physical closeness.

Everything in him wanted to shake off her hand, because the temptation to pull her closer was nearly overwhelming, but he couldn't. Not in the middle of the ballroom with all eyes on them. He'd been the one who'd decided on this lie after all, and changing his mind now would be ridiculous, not to mention an acknowledgment that his control wasn't what it should be.

Shoving away the fierce desire that burned in his blood, Apollo made himself curl his fingers around Flora's, holding on as he stalked towards one particular knot of people.

From then on, the whole evening began to take on the shape of a nightmare.

He couldn't get rid of his intense physical awareness of her. There seemed to be a part of his brain constantly monitoring where exactly she was in relation to him at all times. How close she stood, whether he could smell the sweet scent of her perfume, how the feel of her hand in his made it difficult to think.

Talking to people was almost impossible, since he kept losing his train of thought, and quite often she had to take over the conversation. And perhaps that was the worst thing—or possibly the best, he couldn't decide—because then he had to watch her smile and chat easily to people, charming them, and not with the kind of manipulation his father used, but with a natural effervescent spirit that he'd had no idea she possessed.

It was like realising a previously insignificant daisy was actually a sunflower, and now it was blooming in all its glory, and he couldn't stop staring.

How was this utterly delightful, beautiful woman the same as his impassive, unquestioning PA? In her boring black-and-white PA uniform? Who did everything he said and never complained, never protested?

He watched her now, chatting to the CEO of a global bank, as if she'd known the woman all her life and not only met her seconds ago. The CEO was smiling and laughing, introducing her husband to Flora, totally ignoring Apollo, standing tall and unsmiling beside her.

No, she wasn't his PA tonight. She was wearing his ring. She was his fiancée.

A lull came in the conversation, and abruptly Apollo couldn't stand being in this ballroom with her so close a second longer. Couldn't stand the lie this was, a lie that held a component of truth he couldn't escape.

He wanted her. It was all purely physical, nothing to do with the brightness of her eyes or the brilliance of her smile. It was simply common lust, nothing special, yet he was having difficulty resisting, and that was an issue. He had to get her away from him as quickly as possible.

Gripping her hand tightly, he said to the group at large,

not caring if he was interrupting the conversation, 'If you'll forgive me, we really must be going.'

His words fell into the glittering edifice of the conversation like stones smashing through glass. His voice had come out harsh and blunt, but he didn't bother tempering it. He *was* harsh and blunt, and people could do what they wanted with it.

Everyone stared at him in surprise, and he supposed he should murmur some meaningless platitudes and smile, but he'd never felt less like smiling.

Instead he turned and strode in the direction of the exit without another word, tugging Flora along with him.

'What's wrong?' she asked breathlessly as they came out of the ballroom and into the glittering hallway.

'Nothing.' Pulling his phone out of his pocket, he texted his driver, even as he kept heading for the front doors, his other hand still holding hers and tugging her along. 'It was merely time to leave.'

'Really? Right now? But we've only been here an hour.'

He ignored her, striding outside, continuing to lead her along as he went down the stairs to meet the limo that had just pulled up.

After they'd got inside and the doors had closed, she turned to look at him, concern in her eyes. 'Are you sure you're okay? That was very sudden.'

'You know I don't like events.' His voice was probably too harsh, but he didn't care. 'As I said, it was time to leave.' He was overwhelmingly conscious of her gaze on him. He'd been conscious of it all night. Every time she looked at him, he'd felt it like an electric shock, and it was slowly driving him insane. 'Stop looking at me like that,' he growled, staring straight ahead as the limo pulled away from the kerb.

'Like what?' She sounded bewildered.

Apollo couldn't stand it. He turned and met her silvery gaze, unable to keep himself from glancing at her bare shoulders where her black hair licked like dark flames over the creamy expanse of her skin, before looking back to her face again. 'How do you think?' He snarled the words like a beast.

There was nothing but puzzlement on her face. 'I'm sorry, did I—'

He reached for her before she could finish, suddenly beside himself with frustration as he hauled her into his lap. She didn't make a sound, didn't protest, and when he took her hair in a fist and pulled her head back, she didn't tell him to stop. And when he took her mouth as if he'd been kissing her for years, as if she was his, she opened it, sliding her arms around his neck and clinging onto him for dear life.

This was a terrible idea, and he knew it. He should stop, take his mouth from hers and put her back in her seat, but he didn't.

He leaned forward instead, still kissing her, hitting the button that activated the screen between the driver and the backseat. Then he kissed her deeper, harder. Sliding his tongue into her mouth and exploring, feasting. She was a delectable treat, tasting of all those long-forgotten summers, and he couldn't stop himself from wanting more. He was quite sure he'd never tasted anything as delicious as she was.

Flora gave a soft little moan in the back of her throat, the way she'd done back in the ballroom, and he dug his fingers into the soft black mass of her hair, closing them into fists. Pulling her head back further so he could taste her deeper.

Her body was pliant as warm wax, no resistance in her at all, as if she too had been waiting for this moment between them, as if it had been inevitable, only a matter of time.

And maybe it was. Maybe this chemistry between them had only been hidden, buried and smouldering, waiting for the right moment to catch alight and burn bright.

You were supposed to keep your hands off her.

He was. Now, though, it was too late. He was crossing boundaries he shouldn't be crossing, the self-imposed boundaries he'd put there for the good of his reputation and to protect people. Protect them from him.

But he didn't think he could stop. Certainly not with her fingers tugging at his tie, trying to undo it so she could get at the buttons of his shirt. She kept shifting her weight in his lap, and the pressure against his aching groin was maddening.

He had to do something to stop this, or else he'd fall all the way down that slippery slope to the bottom.

Gathering all his considerable will, Apollo wrenched his mouth away, holding tight to her hair to keep her still. 'This should not happen,' he growled.

Her eyes were black in the dim interior of the limo, her mouth full and red and open as a flower. 'Why not?' Her own voice didn't sound much better than his.

'Because you work for me. Because I'm your boss.'

'So?' She touched his jaw, her fingertips lightly tracing the line of it. 'I don't care if you don't, and everyone thinks we're already sleeping together.'

The caress of her fingers… It made him want to grab her hand, maybe bite her fingertips, nip them, watch her face while he did it and see if she liked it—

No. He had to stop this and now, while he still could. He'd told himself that he wasn't going to touch her, and if he couldn't control simple lust, then what kind of man was he?

The kind who ruins people. The kind who sold out his own father.

'No,' he said flatly, both to her and the voice in his head.

But she ignored him. 'Apollo.' Unexpectedly, she took his chin in her hand, holding him the way he'd held her the day before. 'Look at me.' Her skin was so beautifully flushed, her hair tangled. She looked like a woman well tumbled already, and they hadn't done more than kiss. 'I want you,' she went on. 'I want you badly. And it doesn't have to mean anything, not if we don't want it to. We could just have one night. Just one. We're not hurting anyone, and the next day we'll go back to pretending.'

She let go of his chin, her fingertips sliding down his throat, to where his pulse beat hard, resting there. She didn't look away from him, her eyes a dark sea he could fall into and drown in. 'Please. Please, don't make me beg.'

His control should have been strong enough to resist her. In fact, it should have been easy. But it wasn't and easy was the last thing it was. His brain felt full of treacle, the usual smooth turning of cogs and gears heavy and sticky. It seemed to take a lot of effort to even think why he was supposed to keep his hands off her, especially when something inside him kept straining at the leash he'd put on it, wanting to break free. The wild, reckless part of him, which he'd imprisoned the night he'd picked up the phone and called the police.

One night. What would it hurt? She wanted him. And the way she looked at him, as if she might die if she didn't get to have him, was making him harder than he'd ever been in his entire life.

'One night,' he ground out eventually. 'Just one.'

Her eyes seemed to catch fire then and he couldn't wait. Just couldn't. The leash on his control broke, and he was leaning forward, taking her mouth in a savage kiss before she could speak.

She didn't seem to mind that it wasn't courteous or restrained. She only sighed as if in relief, as if his kiss was cool water on a burn, taking away the pain, making it better. Then her hands resumed their attack on his tie, clawing at the fabric and the shirt buttons beneath it, as hungry for him as he was for her.

She wasn't lying. She *did* want him.

The desire raging inside him had fully broken away and, like the tide, there was nothing he could do to stop it from swamping him. Nothing mattered. Not where they were, not who they were. Nothing except this relentless, aching hunger, and the surge of adrenaline spiking in his blood, flooding him with that familiar recklessness.

He took her hands and pulled them away from him, because that touch of hers was too much, putting them behind her back and imprisoning her wrists in an iron grip. Then he looked straight into her darkened eyes. 'Here,' he demanded. 'Now.'

CHAPTER SIX

His grip was iron. There was no way for her to break it. And the look in his eyes, black in the dim confines of the limo, was fierce, almost savage with hunger.

He was a starving lion and she was his prey, but unlike a poor antelope, she didn't want to get away. She was already caught, and now she wanted him to gorge on her, feast on her until she couldn't bear it any more.

The world had narrowed to the gleam in his eyes, the warm strength of his hands gripping her wrists, the intolerable ache between her thighs.

Her plans were forgotten—she couldn't even remember why getting close to him mattered—and she didn't care.

She didn't care that he was the man who'd caused her father's death, the reason she'd lost her mother too, and why the safe, contented little bubble of her childhood had been shattered.

She didn't even care that the man who'd destroyed so many parts of her life was going to take her virginity.

None of those things seemed important, not any more.

There was only him. Him and his touch, his kiss, the chemistry that sparked and flared in the air around them.

His body was hard beneath hers, like stone, and her mouth felt full and sensitive from the effects of that blinding kiss. Her clothes felt too tight, constraining her, and she wanted to be rid of them. She wanted to be naked, basking in the heat he was putting out, sunning herself like a cat.

Here, he'd said. *Now.*

Of course, here. Of course, now. Those were the only logical answers.

'Yes,' she said hoarsely, her voice cracked as old paint. 'Yes, *please.*'

He shifted her on his lap, levelling that fierce stare at her as he adjusted her, easing her knees apart so they were spread on either side of his hips and she was facing him. He didn't let go of her wrists.

'I'm going to hold you like this.' His voice was soft and rough as frayed velvet, his gaze electric. 'You can't touch me, understand? Not yet.'

She swallowed, her mouth dry, her heart beating so hard she could barely hear anything. 'Why not?'

'Because you've got me on edge like a teenage boy,' he said bluntly.

That thrilled her. So, he wanted her *that* much, did he? That made her feel good, made her feel powerful in a way she hadn't ever felt before. He was a billionaire, head of a vast company, a man known for his iron control and his rigidity, and yet here he was, holding her hands behind her back, because her touch was too much for him. *She* threatened his control, and she liked it.

Her heart raced even faster. What would happen if she *did* touch him? What would happen if he lost his hold on that control of his? A shiver chased over her skin, her thoughts tumbling over themselves.

Oh, she wanted to see that. She wanted to see him totally at the mercy of this chemistry between them. She wanted to see him undone by her touch, by *her*.

This is how he can destroy you...

The thought flickered through her head, so fast she barely noted it. Right now all that seemed important was that glint in his eyes, that fire. She wanted to see it burn higher, burn his control to ash and unleash the passion imprisoned by it. Except, to do that, she needed to touch him and he had her wrists in a grip too strong for her to break.

She'd always been wary of losing control, of feeling helpless against the strength of her own emotions, but she didn't feel helpless now. Even with him holding her wrists. He'd let her go if she wanted, she knew that he would, but she didn't want him to.

She wanted sit just like this and see if he would join her where she was, in the middle of all this delicious fire.

Flora lifted her chin and held his gaze, letting him see what he was doing to her, letting him see the depth of her desire, because there was no need to hide it, not now. And deep in his jungle green eyes, she saw an answering desire leap high.

Oh, he liked watching her, he did. And he thought that,

by holding her wrists, he was the one in charge here. But he wasn't. She was seducing him away from his control, and he didn't even realise it. All she had to do was surrender to him, and he'd follow.

Moving slowly, he reached behind her, to the zip of her gown, drawing it down in a smooth, measured movement. The blue silk parted, cool air washing over her heated skin, and it felt glorious. Then he slid the little sleeves down her arms before pulling the neckline down, exposing her breasts.

She hadn't worn a bra, not with that gown, so there was nothing impeding his view, and she might have felt horribly self-conscious with another man, but she wasn't with another man. She was with Apollo, and as the fire in his eyes leaped even higher, she knew he was utterly at her mercy.

'I told you that you were exquisite,' he murmured, his gaze roving all over her, looking at her as if he couldn't get enough. 'And exquisite you are.'

And she knew it, felt the truth of it deep inside. Right now, sitting here in the limo, on his lap, in his arms, she felt every bit as exquisite as he said she was.

He lifted his free hand, touching her, fingertips brushing lightly over the pulse at the base of her throat, then her collarbones, and down, tracing patterns on her bare skin. She shuddered, her breathing uneven, the light caresses making her skin tighten and prickle, and the ache between her thighs get even worse.

'Do you like this?' That soft, velvety voice of his wasn't cold any longer, or impassive. It was threaded through with a rough heat, a hunger that seemed only to acknowledge what she already knew, that she had him wrapped around her little finger. He would deny her nothing.

His hand dropped down further, cupping one breast. 'Do you like me touching you?'

The heat of his palm against her bare skin was an intense pleasure, drawing a shudder of delight that she didn't even attempt to hide. Then his thumb brushed over her already hard nipple, sending sparks everywhere, tearing a gasp from her.

'Answer me, Flora,' he said with rough insistence.

'Yes,' she managed, the word ending on a gasp as he pinched her nipple gently, sending a pulse of electric pleasure through her entire body. 'Yes... I... I like it.'

His gaze was a deep jungle pool, emeralds glittering at the bottom like sunken treasure. Such beautiful eyes. She wanted to drown in them.

His fingers wandered, teasing her and stroking her, mapping the curves of her body as if he had all the time in the world. But she could see the leash he held on his hunger, and she knew she was testing it. It was going to break soon, and she wanted it to.

'I'm your boss.' His fingers moved lower, finding the helm of her gown and sliding beneath it. 'Does that excite you?'

'Yes,' she whispered, all her guards down, letting him see the truth. 'But it's you who excites me. You always have.'

He found her bare thigh, stroking her skin, a fine net

of sparks radiating from where he touched, prickling all over her. 'Always?' He held her gaze captive as his fingers crept higher, between her thighs, touching her, caressing her. 'Since you started working for me?'

Flora shuddered under his touch, surrendering completely to him. 'Yes,' she whispered. 'Always. Right from the first day.'

An expression she couldn't read flickered across his beautiful face, but there was no denying the glittering flames in his eyes. He liked that she had.

'You hid it well, *matia mou*.' Finding the damp silk of her underwear, he pulled the fabric to one side in a deft movement. 'I would never have guessed.'

She gasped as his fingers found the soft, slick folds between her thighs, exploring, teasing, and the pleasure became so acute the gasp turned into a low moan.

No one had ever touched her there before, though sometimes at night she would touch herself, give herself a fleeting physical pleasure for comfort, when she felt too lonely, the journey she'd undertaken too long. When the quest for justice seemed hollow, like one of those pipe dreams of her father's, and she not worthy, not equal to the task.

What Apollo was doing with his hand, though, was nothing like the feeling when she touched herself. It was sharper and so much more intense that she found herself trembling, on the brink of climax already.

It might have felt too exposing to be so undone by him, to be held helpless like this, trembling under his gaze like that antelope under the paw of a lion, but it didn't feel exposing. And she didn't feel at his mercy or helpless.

No, it was the other way around. *He* was helpless. *He* was at *her* mercy, and she knew it by the savage glitter in his eyes, the way his stare was locked with hers, as if he couldn't look away. As if there was nowhere he'd rather be looking than at her.

He was desperate for her, his forgotten PA. The daughter who hadn't been enough for one parent, and who'd been a millstone around the neck of the other. She had him on his knees with a desire so strong he'd crossed all his own lines, burned his code of ethics to the ground, and overturned his vaunted control so badly he couldn't wait until they got back to the Constantinides residence to have her.

Power coursed through her and she loved it. She loved that look in his eyes and the way he touched her. She felt like a phoenix, rising magnificently from the ashes, golden and brilliant and beautiful, the object of everyone's desire.

But it was his desire that mattered most to her.

And it was time to unleash it.

He stroked her, easing one finger inside her, pressing her wrists into the small of her back with his other hand, making her spine arch, her bare breasts pressing against the cotton of his shirt. She groaned, her head falling back as the pleasure intensified. 'Please…' she murmured. 'Please…'

'Please, what?' His voice was so deep it was a growl, insistent, demanding.

Flora looked at him beneath her lashes, moving restlessly against his hand, watching as the leash he had on his own desire began to loosen. 'Please, sir,' she whispered.

The look in his eyes blazed. 'Good girl.' He eased in another finger, sliding them in and out, a rhythm that had her panting. 'Very good, *matia mou.*' And he kept on watching as his fingers moved, and the wave broke over her, and she cried out, trembling as pleasure swamped her.

She could see him then, still looking at her, staring at her as if he'd suddenly discovered God, and he was so close to the edge. It wouldn't take much to push him over, and she wanted him to.

He'd stripped her of her control, now it was time for her to strip him of his.

'Let me go,' she whispered, and immediately, his hold on her wrists loosened. She shifted on him, hearing the harsh intake of his breath, feeling the hard evidence of his desire beneath her. Not that she needed either to know how close he was to that edge, not when she could see the bonfire in his eyes.

Flora lifted her hands and took his face between them. 'Now, sir,' she murmured, meeting his gaze. 'Let yourself go.'

Flora had done something to him and he didn't know what it was. What he did know was that he couldn't think, couldn't move, could barely breathe from the intensity of the desire flooding him.

He felt strung out, almost wild, only hanging on to his control by the skin of his teeth. One slip and that grip would break, and he had no idea what would happen if it did.

Yet looking up in her passion-darkened eyes, the sweet smell of her body and her arousal all around him, the top of her gown down around her waist, and her bare skin warm, he was starting not to care.

What did it matter if he did? He'd barely managed to keep it together as he'd slowly uncovered her, unwrapping her like a present, and touching her, caressing her lovely body, had driven him to the edge. Perhaps he shouldn't have told her what she did to him, perhaps he shouldn't have admitted it. Then again, he knew she'd liked his desire for her, knew that it had added to her pleasure, and watching her react to him had been the sweetest gift.

She'd let him see everything, had held nothing back, and something in him had responded to abandon. The reckless, wild part of him that he had to keep under control was fighting to be set free.

She had seen that too, and now with her whispering to him to let go, he couldn't think of anything he wanted to do more.

Apollo forgot about the slippery slope. Forgot that he needed to keep that part of himself under wraps. Forgot everything but the savagery of the desire inside him, and how he needed to bury it in the woman who'd set it free.

There was no time for niceties. No time for gentleness or care. He pulled out his wallet, found himself a condom, then jerked the buttons of his trousers open. It didn't take more than a moment to sheath himself, before he was gripping her hips, positioning her where he wanted her.

He kept his gaze on hers as he lifted her, then eased her down onto him, pushing into the tight, slick heat of her body. Her eyes went wide and her mouth opened, her hitching gasp echoing the limo.

Beautiful, beautiful woman.

He wanted to stay like this, buried inside her, watching the pleasure climb in her eyes the way he had just before, but the demands of his body were too much. He couldn't stop his hips from lifting, couldn't stop his hands from tightening on her, holding her firmly in place as he drove himself into her.

'Sir…' she whispered, the pleasure-soaked sound of the word adding a forbidden spice to his own desire. 'Oh… Apollo…'

Yes, and his name too, spoken just like that… So good…

He couldn't drag his gaze from her face, all delicately flushed, her hair a black tangle around her shoulders, her grey eyes darkened into black. He'd undone her, his unflappable little PA. He'd made her moan, and now he was going to make her scream.

He drove deeper, her gasps of pleasure music to his ears, and yet also loosening his grip on his own sanity. He wanted to make her come again, but he wasn't sure he could hold on long enough. He'd never had that problem before, never.

She will be the ruin of you.

The thought was there and then it was gone before he'd had a chance to fully grasp it. But by then he didn't care. All that mattered was the tight heat of her body, the way she moaned, the endless darkness of her eyes.

Everything had narrowed.

He didn't care that they were in his limo having sex.

He didn't care that she was his PA.

He didn't care about his reputation or his name.

What he cared about was making her come before the climax claimed him too, so he pushed his hand between them, his fingers sliding between her legs to where she was most sensitive, and he stroked her, giving her some added friction.

Flora cried out, her back arching, her head going back as the climax hit her, and he reached for her then, plunging his fingers into her hair and dragging her mouth down onto his, moving harder, faster, his hips falling out of rhythm as the orgasm took him as well. The kiss turned savage and he said her name over and over against her mouth, as the pleasure took him like a building collapsing on top of him.

He wasn't sure how long it took for him to come back to himself. Perhaps an age, perhaps mere seconds, but for a while he was somewhere else. Somewhere far away, where there was nothing in the world but the woman in his arms, her sweetness, her heat, the tight grip of her sex around his. Her soft moans, her needy cries, the abandon with which she'd given herself to him.

He wasn't even Apollo Constantinides, imprisoned

on all sides by the boundaries he'd put around himself, or the rigid control he'd kept himself under.

No, he was just a man with a woman he desired, and who desired him in return. Nothing more, but certainly nothing less. And it was a strange thing, but in the afterglow of the most intense climax he'd ever had, he felt as if he'd been suffocating for years, and only now could he finally breathe.

It was Flora. It was all her. How she'd known he'd been holding himself back, he had no idea, but when she'd told him to let go, he had, as if he'd been waiting for the chance to do so all this time and had never dared. Letting the wildness take him and following it wherever it led and… She'd joined him there.

He'd never let himself go like that with a woman before, never ever, and now that he had… Well, now, he felt more like himself than he could remember feeling for a long, long time.

A night, though. That's all you have.

Flora had collapsed forward onto him, her head on his shoulder, and he put a hand to the back of her head, feeling the softness of her hair under his palm. Feeling the softness of her body, warm and relaxed, pressed to his.

A night he'd said, but that had been before she'd completely decimated his control. And she had. Which meant she was a dangerous woman.

Apollo glanced down at her, feeling her soft breaths against his neck. Her eyes were closed, lashes lying softly on her pink cheeks.

He should get rid of her, he knew that. He should perhaps transfer her to a different position in the company, where she wasn't working directly with him, where she could never threaten his command over himself again. And if he hadn't spent years polishing the Constantinides name, making his reputation the pillar upon which everything stood, he might have done just that, ending this pretence of an engagement as well.

But he couldn't.

Everyone thought they were sleeping together, as she'd already pointed out, so maybe they should make that part of it real. That wouldn't break anything. In fact, now that he thought about it, maybe sleeping together would be a good thing. The hold he'd had on himself had been too rigid, but if he could let go with her, within the confines of a bed and, very soon, marriage vows, then that would be a good way for him to let off steam. Indulge his recklessness physically, with a woman who matched him.

Satisfaction gathered inside him as he leaned back against the seat, cradling Flora in his arms. She didn't move, seemingly content to lie there against him.

Yes, that's what he'd do. He'd marry her quickly, make her his wife, and then, once this chemistry between them had burned itself out, they'd go their separate ways, her reputation and his safely intact.

Having sex with Flora wasn't the slippery slope back down to the man he'd once been, it just wasn't. Too many years had passed of him being who he was now, years of having those boundaries around him, years of making sure his moral compass pointed true north.

He would never be that young man again, hungry for

his father's approval, proud of his business skills and the way he could charm people, the way he could get them to do anything he wanted. He'd enjoyed bending people to his will back then, seducing them into giving him all their money, it had given him the purest thrill. And then seeing his father look at him as if Apollo was his golden child.

He'd told the police, the media, his mother, he'd told anyone who asked that he hadn't known what his father was doing. That he hadn't seen the signs that his father's investment scheme wasn't as legitimate as it had appeared. That he was just as much a victim of his father's machinations as everyone else was...

But, deep down, there was a truth he hadn't wanted to acknowledge.

He'd known. He'd known exactly what his father had been doing, and he hadn't cared. It had been the first time his father had brought him in, and he'd been too excited to be working with him, to finally be at his side in the family business, that he'd ignored the signs. Ignored the instinct in his gut that had told him there was something amiss.

He'd been chasing that thrill with reckless abandon, loving how his father would drape his arm around Apollo's neck and tell him how proud he was of him. What a chip off the old block he was. All he'd ever wanted to be at that moment in time was his father, his hero.

Now, all he wanted was to be different.

And he was. Sex with Flora wouldn't change things, it just wouldn't.

He wound his fingers into her hair and tilted her head to the side, looking down at her. Black hair covered his jacket, the rosy pink of her cheek contrasting against his white shirt.

Pretty, pretty Flora.

'Are you okay, *matia mou*?' he murmured, the endearment coming as easily as it had before they'd had sex.

She let out a long and very satisfied sigh. 'Yes, I'm very okay.' She glanced up at him, grey eyes still darkened with pleasure. 'You are quite incredible, do you know that?'

'So I've been told. On a number of occasions.'

She smiled, pure amusement glittering in her gaze, and his heart skipped a beat. She was so relaxed like this, lying against him as if she'd done it all her life, looking up at him as if she truly loved him, as if this wasn't a sham at all, but entirely real. She was a woman who was freer and more natural, more passionate and sparkling than his buttoned-up, impassive PA. There was also a mischievousness to her, a glint of something wicked in her eyes, which sparked an answering wickedness in him.

'You're so arrogant,' she said, as if this was an utterly delightful quality.

And he couldn't stop the smile that turned his mouth. A rare smile, since he'd never found that there was much about life to smile at. But he did so now, because she was beautiful, and the way she looked at him made him feel as if there were things to smile about now. 'And you like it,' he said, his fingers playing through her hair, loving the feel of it against his skin. 'You certainly liked calling me "sir".'

Colour swept over her skin, her eyes glinting silver. 'Maybe. Or maybe I just like to indulge your dominating tendencies.'

'That's good, because I have a lot of those tendencies.'

'So I've noticed.' The smile faded from her face slowly. 'So…this is probably a bit late now, but what's going to happen after tonight?'

He shifted her into a more comfortable position. 'Do you want more?' It was a question he thought he knew the answer to, but he wanted her to say it.

'Yes,' she said honestly, obliging him. 'You must know I do.'

'Then you shall have it.' He pushed a strand of hair back behind her ear. 'I propose a wedding as quickly as possible, and then you will move in with me. We'll have a proper marriage for as long as we both want it.'

'Move in with you?' She raised an imperious brow. 'Perhaps you need to move in with me.'

She was teasing him, he thought, but he liked it. He liked it very much indeed. However, he realised, as soon as she said it, that he didn't know where she lived. Or if she lived alone. Presumably she wasn't with anyone, otherwise she wouldn't have had sex with him. No, he was sure she wouldn't, but…

You don't know anything about her.

Something cold penetrated the warmth in his gut, sitting uncomfortably sharp inside him, though he wasn't sure why. Flora had passed all the background checks his

HR department did on every employee, and she'd never lied to him. She wasn't a dishonest person, he was sure.

How would you know, when you never paid any attention to her?

His fingers tightened in her hair. 'And where do you live, hmm?' He kept his voice light, matching hers.

'I live in a bedsit. You'd probably find it a bit…small.'

That struck him oddly. He paid her a very good wage, yet she could only afford a bedsit? 'Why?' he asked, abruptly curious. 'I know how much I pay you. You could afford better.'

She sniffed. 'It's a very nice bedsit, actually. But you know, London prices.'

He did know. There were a number of charities he was personally involved with that were trying to tackle homelessness, so he was aware of the issues.

'Yes, but I'm sorry, I'm not moving into your bedsit.' He kept his tone dry. 'You'll have to live with me. At least for the duration of our marriage.'

'Oh, no,' she said plaintively. 'I'll have to move in with my billionaire husband. Whatever shall I do?' The tension had drained out of her, and there was an amused glint in her eye that had his body hardening again.

Pretty Flora.

'A terrible situation indeed,' he murmured, stroking her cheek. 'You might simply have to bear it by lying back and thinking of England.'

Her mouth curved the way it had done earlier that evening, in the ballroom, and he felt savagely pleased with himself that he'd got a smile from her. 'If you have anything to do with it, I won't be able to think at all.'

'That's the plan,' he said, and kissed her.

CHAPTER SEVEN

FLORA WOKE UP the next morning, her body aching in all sorts of unfamiliar places. It wasn't a bad thing, though. In fact, she felt deliciously sated and delightfully lazy, like a cat after consuming a whole saucer of cream.

She rolled over in the massive bed, which Apollo had carried her to the night before, and reached for him.

Only to find the other side of the bed empty.

Frowning, she sat up and looked around the spacious bedroom, but that was empty too.

Thrown across the end of the bed, though, was a swathe of white silk, which on further inspection proved to be the prettiest dressing gown Flora had ever seen. Her clothes seemed to have vanished—she couldn't even remember what had happened to them after she and Apollo had arrived at the house the evening before. Apollo had hurried her from the limo, taking her in his arms the moment the big front doors had closed behind them, and then…

Well, then nothing had seemed to matter, except them both being naked together, with nothing between them but warm, bare skin.

He hadn't been controlled then and neither had she. The leash she'd taken off him in the limo had remained firmly off the whole night, and it had been the most incredible, wild experience she'd ever had. He was an insatiable, inventive lover, indulging her and himself in a few sensual domination games that she'd absolutely loved.

She'd had no idea that sex could be like that. That it could be so consuming, so addictive and, yes, addictive was exactly the word she'd use to describe sex with Apollo. Part of her had wondered if it had been amazing because she'd never had sex before, but then...

It's not that. It's because of him.

Flora closed her eyes, her head full of memories of the night before.

He'd been demanding and hungry, but also gentle, as if he'd been aware of her inexperience. And of course he must have been. He'd had to guide her a few times, and had done so with a patience that belied the hunger he'd shown her in the limo, not to mention a certain tenderness that had made her chest ache.

She hadn't had tenderness from anyone since her mother had died, and she'd had no idea Apollo could be both patient and tender. In fact, there appeared to be a few things about Apollo Constantinides that she hadn't anticipated, and she wasn't sure how she felt about that.

This could end up backfiring on you if you're not careful.

Oh, it could. But she wouldn't let it. Losing control in bed was not the same thing as losing control of her emotions, and those she was holding very tightly.

Anyway, luckily, after the question about where she lived, he hadn't asked her anything else about herself. No, he'd had other things on his mind, and talking was not one of them.

However, she knew he'd probably ask them at some point, in which case she'd better have a few easy lies on hand to give him.

Still thinking about it, Flora opened her eyes again, threw back the sheet and slid out of bed. Then she picked up the dressing gown and wrapped it around her naked body. The silk was cool against her skin, the most delightful indulgence.

She never allowed herself pretty things. Everything she did was in service to her plans. He'd seemed surprised the night before when she'd told him she lived in a bedsit, and given the amount of money he paid her, he might very well be surprised. But she'd put all that money into a savings account; she wanted to have some funds to help her disappear once she'd finished her heartbreak plans.

Tying her robe closed, Flora then opened the door and stepped out into the ornate hallway outside. It was empty, so she went along to the stairs that led down into the main entrance of the house. As she went down them, she heard voices coming from below. One voice was very familiar, and her heart gave the oddest little leap.

Apollo was standing in the entrance way, talking in French to an older looking man dressed in black. Apollo himself was in dark trousers and a white shirt, the sleeves rolled up and his hair slightly mussed, and he seemed to sense her approach, because he suddenly broke off his conversation and glanced in the direction of the stairs where she stood.

His eyes glittered as he took her in, and even though the white silk was very decorous, she abruptly felt as if she wasn't wearing anything at all.

'Good morning, *matia mou*,' he said. 'Come, I want to introduce you to someone.'

She came down the rest of the stairs, and when he took her hand and drew her in close, one arm sliding around her waist, she didn't protest. Then she noticed that the other man was wearing a dog collar.

'This is Father Bayard,' Apollo said. 'He is going to marry us.'

She couldn't mask the ripple of shock that went through her, and Apollo must have felt her instinctively stiffen, because he said something in French to the priest, who nodded and went past them in the direction of the back of the house.

Flora could hear voices coming from that direction too. It sounded as if orders were being given.

'You can't mean we're getting married today,' she said, and didn't make it a question since the very idea seemed preposterous.

One of those addictive, fascinating smiles lurked in the corner of Apollo's mouth. '*Mais oui.* Indeed we are getting married today.'

Flora blinked. 'But—'

'I know,' he interrupted gently. 'I should have spoken to you about this earlier, but I had arrangements to make, and you needed the sleep.' His eyes glinted. 'I was not exactly restrained last night.'

As if she needed the reminder.

'No, you weren't,' she said, her cheeks feeling hot. 'Not that I was complaining. But…a wedding? Now? Today? I thought you wanted a spectacle.'

'I thought I did too. But last night was…' His smile turned warm, deepening that ache in her chest. 'A revelation. So, I thought, like I told you in the limo, that getting married as quickly as possible would be the best thing all round.' He pulled her closer, the heat of his body burning through the silk, making her knees feel weak. 'Also, given the level of media interest in you, the sooner we're married, the sooner you'll be protected. Plus, this will add credence to ours being a grand passion. We couldn't wait to be married, so we had a quick wedding on the terrace outside. I've already got someone from PR to take a few informal photos that can be leaked to the press.'

Flora blinked again, feeling as if she'd somehow got on a rollercoaster and now couldn't get off. No, wait, this had to be a good thing. He was right, it would look very romantic if they had a quick wedding today, and it would certainly be in her interests too. The less time the press had to be curious about her the better, and, anyway, once she was married to him, even if her links to his father's scheme did come out, he might find it difficult to get rid of her. Also, he still wouldn't know her real reasons for getting close to him. If and when he eventually did, with any luck he'd be so wrapped around her little finger, it might not even bother him.

Do you seriously think it won't bother him that you've been lying to him?

No, she knew it would. He'd never made any secret of the fact that he didn't like a liar. But if the sex was good enough, and she'd already managed to get under his guards emotionally, he might, after a few days of being angry, come round. After all, it wasn't as if she knew nothing about how to deal with him. She'd been working with him for a year, and while he wasn't an easy man, she'd developed a few little strategies to handle him.

Apollo frowned all of a sudden and abruptly lifted his hands, cupping her face between them. 'You seem uncertain. Is this too fast? Do you have family that should be invited? I could fly them over here if you wish, and we could wait until then.'

The mention of family caught her off-guard. 'Family?' she echoed blankly.

'Yes. I know this wedding is still a pretence, but it will look strange, I suppose, if your family isn't here.'

Flora took a silent breath, trying to think of an appropriate response. The truth was the easiest. The best lies, after all, were always based on some aspect of the truth. She just wouldn't mention her father's name. she'd tell Apollo he'd died in a car accident or something.

'I have no family,' she said, trying not to avoid his gaze. 'My father died when I was a kid, and my mother died a few years ago. Cancer. I'm an only child.'

Something shifted in his gaze, though she couldn't tell what it was. Sympathy perhaps? It seemed strange to get sympathy from Apollo Constantinides.

'I'm sorry for your loss, Flora,' he said, and yes, it *was* sympathy she could hear in his voice. 'That must have been very hard.'

Inexplicably, the backs of her eyes prickled. It had been a long time since anyone had said anything comforting to her, as if they genuinely felt for her. The nurses at the hospital had been very kind, but also a touch impersonal.

Now, though, with Apollo cupping her face in his hands, understanding in his green eyes... There was nothing impersonal about this. Nothing fake, either. He was being utterly genuine.

Unlike you.

Guilt tugged inside her, unexpected and painfully sharp. He was being understanding and kind, while she was...

Just a liar.

Her chest felt tight, but she pushed the sensation away. She had to keep going. She *had* to. Her father might have done the most senseless thing she could imagine, and she had to acknowledge her own anger at him for that. Anger that he hadn't stayed to be there for her and her mother. Anger that he hadn't kept all the promises he'd made.

But he wouldn't have been in that position if not for the man standing in front of her now. She needed some justice for her father, and Apollo Constantinides's broken heart would have to do.

'It was,' she managed.

'I lost my parents too.' His thumbs brushed her cheek. 'Though I was an adult when they died. It's harder to lose a parent when you're a child.'

Was that grief she saw in his eyes? For his father? Or was it for his mother?

Not that she was curious. His losses were nothing in comparison to hers, and she had to remember that, no matter how understanding he might sound.

'I was ten when Dad died,' she heard herself say, even though she could have sworn she wasn't going to give him anything more. 'My mother and I were left with nothing, so she had to work really hard to keep a roof over our heads. She thought she was so tired was from working all the time, but…it wasn't that at all.'

Apollo frowned slightly.

God, what on earth had made her say that to him? What an idiot she was being. She was supposed to give him a grain of truth and then lie about the rest, not the truth wholesale. She couldn't afford to give him anything more.

'Sorry,' she said quickly. 'That's not exactly great wedding-day conversation.'

'You don't need to apologise,' he murmured. 'I would love to know more.'

That wasn't what she wanted to hear. She needed to change the subject and quickly.

'Later,' she said lightly. 'Don't we have a wedding to go to?'

Apollo's frown lingered, as if he was fully aware of her avoidance. 'We will revisit this, *matia mou*.'

Her stomach tightened. Great. Him being curious about her was the last thing she needed.

'Sure.' She shoved the flutter of nerves aside, keeping her tone easy.

'Good.' His frown cleared and he dropped his hands from her face. 'Come. The priest will be waiting for us.'

Apollo stood on the terrace of his family's French chateau, in the brilliant Parisian sunlight, the roses around the terrace filling the warm air with their heady scent, and watched Flora walk slowly over to where he stood.

She wore the lovely white silk dressing gown he'd bought especially for her—the quickest way he could get a wedding dress—and her black hair was loose around her shoulders. In her hands she carried a bouquet of roses she'd picked from the garden, and a delicate flush stained her cheekbones.

She really was the loveliest woman he'd ever seen.

The night before had been… Well, the best of his life, if he was being honest with himself, and he always tried to be. In bed, she'd been amazing. Inexperienced, he'd thought, but hungry too, welcoming everything he'd done to her, and then not just welcoming, but issuing her own demands in return. She'd been passionate and honest and generous, holding nothing back from him. He'd never had a lover like her.

He'd woken up that morning with her beside him, and in that moment he'd known that he absolutely had to make her his wife as soon as possible. Yes, it was to protect her, but also—and this he couldn't deny—there was an element of possessiveness in his desire for her.

He wanted her to be his wife because he wanted her to be his. His and *only* his.

For a limited time only, of course, but he didn't see why they couldn't start that time as soon as possible.

No one, surely, would raise an eyebrow at a very quick wedding. It would even look romantic if the appropriate story was put in place. They needn't have a spectacle. All they needed was a few leaked photos of Flora looking charming, and himself looking pleased, and that would handle any rumours.

He'd managed to handle the logistics fairly quickly, expediting a marriage licence and getting the rings— simple platinum bands—from a jeweller he did business with. Nothing was a problem when large sums of money were involved.

Breaking the news to Flora had been the most concerning part, since it had only been last night that they'd first slept together, and he wondered if she would find it all a little rushed. When she'd come downstairs as he was talking to the priest—in that white robe and her beautiful hair in a tangle—he'd even found himself thinking that if she said no to him now, maybe he could elope with her somewhere else, take some time to convince her that this was a good strategy.

But he needn't have worried. She'd been surprised but had agreed to his plan, and now here she was, walking to him where he stood with the priest.

She would be his wife.

The thought made something heavy and satisfied shift inside him, in a way it hadn't with Violet. With Violet he'd discussed every aspect of a marriage, and he'd known exactly what it would be. It wasn't the same with Flora, and yet…somehow the not knowing how a marriage with her would be was…exhilarating. Exciting almost. Like a mystery he couldn't wait to start solving.

He knew nothing about her, except what she'd told him about her family, and as they'd stood in the hallway, echoes of an old grief in her eyes, he realised that they had a few things in common. He too, had lost his parents. He too, was an only child.

What more did they share? What other things did he not know? He wanted to find out as soon as possible.

Flora smiled as she came to stand beside him, and together they faced the priest.

He would take things slow, though. He wouldn't demand everything from her immediately. He had two weeks of events and business meetings in various parts of the globe, and Flora would come with him. They could spend time together, getting to know one another, building the facade of a loving marriage to the public, while exploring their physical hunger for each other in private. It was the best of both worlds, really, and he couldn't have hoped for a better outcome.

The priest began the wedding ceremony and Apollo nodded to the staff member standing with the housekeeper, who was here as a witness. The man took out his phone and began taking unobtrusive pictures.

Soon Apollo was sliding the ring onto Flora's finger and she was doing the same for him, smiling up at him as she did so. And for some reason the fact that this was a sham, that this wasn't actually real, seemed…strange to him.

It *wasn't* real, he knew that intellectually, and yet a current of anticipation was running through him, a degree of excitement that he hadn't felt for a long time.

Perhaps it was the sex. Or perhaps it was that she was his PA and not a stranger to him, that he'd known her and worked with her for at least a year, but it felt as if getting married to her was almost…right.

He couldn't imagine, for example, standing here with Violet.

The priest pronounced them husband and wife, and then it was over. Apollo pulled her close and kissed her, while the designated photographer took some more pictures.

Then he raised his head and dismissed everyone, before taking Flora in his arms and carrying her inside.

'What are you so impatient for?' she asked, laughing as she threw the bouquet of flowers at the housekeeper on their way past. 'Don't tell me, I can guess.'

He approached the stairs and started up them, Flora all warm and silky in his arms. He gave her a wolfish smile. 'I'm sure you can. That is, if you're not too sore from last night.'

She was blushing again. It was delightful. 'Should I be sore?'

They reached the top of the stairs and he began walking down the hallway. 'You might be,' he said as they came to the bedroom. He walked through the doorway, then kicked the door shut behind them. 'Tell me, have you had many lovers, *matia mou*?'

A strange expression crossed her face. 'Oh…uh…not many, no.'

Apollo crossed to the bed, putting her carefully down on the edge of it. She was still blushing and a thought suddenly struck him. Her hesitancy. How she blushed. How he'd had to guide her…

'Flora,' he said. 'Have you in fact had *any* lovers?'

She looked up at the ceiling for a moment, then glanced at him. 'No,' she said at last. 'No, I haven't.'

A ripple of surprise went through him. 'You were a virgin last night?'

She let out a breath. 'Yes.'

Apollo didn't care how many lovers a woman had had. It didn't matter to him. And yet… Flora the night before, in the limo, he'd been demanding, rough…

'You should have told me,' he said, suddenly concerned. 'I would have been more gentle with you.'

'Honestly?' Flora's gaze this time was level. 'I forgot all about it. You made me feel so good that it just didn't matter.'

At that, something in his chest tightened. He wasn't a man who generally made people feel good. He *did* good, but that was different. Doing good implied some distance. Doing good wasn't specific or personal. Just as caring for humanity in general wasn't the same as caring for a person.

He didn't want to care for an actual person. He'd done

that once before, and it had led him to make the worst mistake of his life. He wasn't willing to do it again.

Except…it was important for him to make Flora feel good. That *was* personal.

Unless she's lying to you. That's happened before, remember?

Oh, yes, he remembered. The conviction in his father's voice when he'd told Apollo that there was nothing wrong with the scheme. His outrage when it was suggested that the scheme was illegal. The glow of approval in his eyes when Apollo had convinced yet another poor sap to invest his money…

No. That approval was real. And you liked it.

Apollo shoved the thought away. His father was dead and gone now, and he wasn't going to put his suspicions on Flora.

'I'm told it can hurt,' he said, crouching in front of her and scanning her face.

'Perhaps for some people it might. But there was no pain for me.' She gave him a heartbreakingly lovely smile, the truth plain in her eyes. Then she reached out and ruffled his hair. 'Truly, none at all. I wondered if last night was so amazing because sex is amazing, but now I think it was just because of you.'

The tightness in his chest squeezed, a strange kind of ache.

Dear God, he could get used to this. To someone looking at him the way she was looking at him right now, as if he'd performed some kind of miracle for her and her alone. To her touching him as a lover of years might, with gentleness and care, as if he mattered to her.

It shouldn't be important to him. This marriage was all a pretence for the sake of their separate reputations, and yet... She'd done everything he'd asked, going way above and even beyond the call of duty.

She was something special, Flora McIntyre. And he hadn't known quite how special until now.

Reaching up, he took her hand from his hair, turned it palm up and pressed a kiss in the centre of it. 'I will take that, wife.' He rose and gently pressed her back onto the bed, reaching for the tie of her gown. 'Now, let me show you how good I can really make you feel.'

CHAPTER EIGHT

FLORA ROLLED OVER in the massive bed, propped her chin on her folded hands and stared out through the huge floor-to-ceiling windows. An afternoon thunderstorm was moving in over the skyscrapers of Hong Kong.

She and Apollo had arrived late the night before, after a charity event in New York, and had come straight to the luxury Victoria Peak apartment he owned. He had some business with the Helios Hong Kong office that he was going to take care of, before they went on to Athens and his property in Greece.

Two weeks had passed since their marriage on the terrace of that house in Paris, not a long time, yet Flora felt as if the entire course of her life had shifted.

The afternoon after the ceremony, still lying in bed together, they'd drafted various press releases and sent them off, detailing how in love they were, so much so that they hadn't been able to wait to marry, and so had had a quick wedding in the chateau's garden.

That had caused a stir, naturally enough. The press had been full of speculation as to why Apollo had married his PA so quickly, and for a few days there had been a lot of chatter and rumour on social media and in the gossip columns about the possibility of a pregnancy. There were other rumours too and, as she'd feared, they were largely about her. She was a gold digger, some people said, she was blackmailing him, she was a home-wrecker and they'd never give up fighting for 'ViLo'.

There was nothing she could do about that but hope no one enquired too deeply into her background. Apollo, though, had been as good as his word. So far, he'd protected her from the press, shielding her from intrusive questions and instructing his security to make sure the photographers were kept at bay whenever they were out.

She hadn't known he could be so protective, and there was a part of her who loved it. Who loved him holding her hand in his, his tall powerful figure shielding hers as they arrived at whatever event they had next. He was her bulwark against all threats and, even though she knew it was all an act, it made her feel in some small way cared for.

Apollo hadn't broken his promises to her the way her father had. Apollo had told her he'd protect her, and he had.

He'd also done some phone interviews, firmly denying all the pregnancy, blackmail and gold-digger rumours, stating that the hastiness of their marriage was due to love, that was all.

Naturally, she tried to ignore the media circus, but every day she couldn't stop herself from religiously checking websites, message boards and other social media every morning, looking for any mention of her family history. So far, nothing had been said, but she didn't imagine that would last. Someone, somewhere would find out, and she didn't want to think about what would happen then. The now was where she wanted to be, because the now was so good. So…so good.

Since that night in the limo, where she'd jumped into the deep end of her desire, she'd let herself sink deeper and deeper. And instead of drowning, she'd found that she could breathe. That, in fact, it was her element, that she belonged there, and she belonged there with him, because it was his element too.

He was a revelation to her, his blunt honesty allowing her to be honest as well. In the fragile structure of lies she'd built around herself, there was one precious truth, glowing like a pearl. The truth that she was obsessed with him, that she wanted him. That she might be lying to him, but there was nothing fake about the physical passion he managed to draw from her.

It felt freeing to finally be allowed to have this one thing that wasn't a lie.

He hasn't just rocked your world. He's knocked it off its axis entirely.

She let out a sigh, watching as the rain began to pelt against the glass, the skyscrapers across the bay wreathed in cloud.

Being his wife rather than his PA these past two weeks had been…amazing. And not for the parade of glittering events or the endless supply of beautiful gowns and jewels, the jet-setting around on private planes to different countries, or meeting famous celebrities and important political figures.

No, it was him.

Since that night in Paris, he'd taken the chains off the raw passion that lay at the heart of him, and allowed it free rein. It thrilled her that she was the one who'd managed to unleash it, that she, the blank slate of a PA with no experience of men, had been the one to draw it from him.

Ever since the death of her mother, she'd had nothing in her life but that one goal—to bring Apollo down. Everything she did was in service to that goal. She did nothing for herself, nothing that wouldn't ultimately get her what she wanted, which was his utter ruination.

She'd been so one-eyed, so rigid in her pursuit, that she hadn't allowed herself even the smallest of pleasures. Yet, for the past two weeks, pleasures both big and small had crept into her days, and it was all due to him.

There were small acts of care, such as the coffee he brought her every morning once he'd discovered she liked a cup before she got out of bed. Strong and milky, with one sugar.

The warm bath he insisted on drawing for her whenever they were in a new city and she was tired and jet-lagged. He'd let her have some relaxation time before her favourite part, which was when he joined her. She loved his hands on her, washing her back and then her hair, which he took his time over, since he liked washing it, as much as she liked him washing it. He'd also figured out her favourite foods and made sure that they were always available, wherever they were.

Those were the small pleasures, ones she hadn't had since she was a child and her parents were still alive. Part of her knew she should tell him that he didn't need to be so solicitous of her, that this wasn't a real marriage after all, yet another part of her was hungry for it. She had been on her own for so long, she hadn't realised how lonely she'd been until him.

Rain fell across the skyscrapers in a glittering veil.

Flora watched it idly, wondering if she could somehow convince Apollo that they didn't need to go to the party they were supposed to attend that evening. That maybe they could stay here and have a private dinner in bed instead.

This isn't real, remember?

No, it wasn't, but part of it was. And she wanted that part to keep on going for ever.

How can it? When all of this, everything you're doing with him, is built on a lie?

Her heart tightened, the threads of guilt that had subtly woven themselves around it constricting painfully. She'd ignored those threads, told herself she didn't feel them, told herself she was justified in what she was planning to do to him, and yet…

Those were lies too.

But what else was there for her? She could tell him the truth—and part of her desperately wanted to, yet, if she did, it would render the entirety of her life since her mother had died, meaningless. Her parents' deaths meaningless too, and she couldn't let that happen. What was the point of anything otherwise?

Apollo came into the room just then, completely naked and carrying a tray, and Flora forgot about the guilt aching in her heart, watching him instead. He was so much more fascinating, especially when he wore nothing but his smooth, velvety olive skin.

A sigh escaped her. The man truly was the personification of the god he was named for. Broad-shouldered, his chest powerful, his stomach flat and hard, not an ounce of fat on him. Then lower, his narrow hips and muscular thighs, and the glory of that very male part of him.

He put the tray down on the edge of the bed, and she saw he'd brought her a little tasting plate of different cheeses, crackers, grapes and nuts, along with a couple of flutes of champagne.

A traitorous warmth expanded in her chest, the way it always did when he brought things for her, tugging hard on those threads around her heart, deepening the ache. She didn't want to feel this way about him, she couldn't. It was dangerous, and yet she couldn't seem to stop herself from feeling it.

And the more time she had with him, the more of him she wanted, because a curiosity had taken root inside her. About the reasons he was so rigidly controlled on the outside, yet so passionate and hot on the inside.

A forbidden curiosity. She couldn't ask him about himself, because then it might prompt him to ask ques-

tions about her, and that she couldn't allow. Lies were
all she had for him, and she didn't want to tell any more,
not when the weight of the ones she'd already told were
getting heavier by the day.

It was a pity, because he was such an intelligent man,
and they'd had some fascinating conversations. Their
topics had ranged from global politics to books, art and
then onto philosophy, and from there his charity work
and how the rate of scientific progress should be used to
improve the lives of everyone, not just the few. He had
a voracious curiosity, his mind full of knowledge on the
most obscure topics, and she loved talking to him about
them. It was a little depressing that she couldn't recip-
rocate with her own interests, because she really didn't
have any. Her life had always begun and ended with her
quest for justice.

'For me?' she asked, glancing at the tray of food and
smiling as he sat down on the bed beside her.

'You have to keep your strength up for the event tonight.' He slid a propriety hand into her hair and gave her
a hot, slow kiss before releasing her, desire still glittering
in his eyes. 'Not to mention for afterwards.'

She'd never get tired of that look, or the hunger in it,
the desire that was for her and her alone.

*Will he still want you when he finds out who you re-
ally are?*

Flora shoved the thought away, along with the feeling
of foreboding that came along with it. She should have
spent this past week putting a plan in place for what she'd
do if and when the truth came out, how she'd deal with

it, or more specifically how she'd deal with him. But she hadn't. Some part of her simply couldn't bear to think about it, because she just wanted this for a little while. Someone's touch on her skin. Someone's hand to hold. Someone to hold her.

No, not someone. Him.

If you're not careful, it won't be his heart you break. It will be your own.

Apollo frowned, studying her face. 'Are you all right, *matia mou*? You've gone pale.'

She forced another smile, hoping he wouldn't press the issue. 'Only a headache.'

He reached out and cupped her cheek in one of his large, warm hands. 'Shall I get you some painkillers?'

The warmth inside her turned bittersweet. He was a naturally caring man, and very protective, and his concern was absolutely genuine. Yet it wasn't specific to her, she suspected. He would do this for anyone.

You want it to be for you, though.

No. No, she didn't. He was the enemy, and she couldn't lose sight of that.

'No,' she murmured, unable to resist leaning into the warmth of his hand. 'I'm fine, honestly.'

But his frown didn't lift, his gaze narrowing as he scanned her face. 'The last two weeks have been something of a whirlwind, I know. Once we get to Athens, it'll be better.' His thumb brushed her cheekbone gently. 'You could probably do with some rest.'

She hadn't asked him much about what was going to happen after this. He'd mentioned her moving in with him back in Paris, but they hadn't discussed it since. In fact, they hadn't had any practical discussions at all. 'And after that?' she asked, shivering a little as he caressed her again.

'After that, we'll have some time in Greece, then we'll go back to London, and I'll arrange for you to move into my residence there.'

She should leave the future to take care of itself, not ask him anything more, and yet she couldn't stop herself. 'What will happen then? Will I go back to being your PA? Or will you hire someone else?'

His frown deepened. 'Being my PA won't be appropriate now, even with the marriage. I know I promised you that your job wouldn't be affected by our arrangement, and it won't be. But perhaps you might feel more comfortable in another position?'

She hadn't thought of a different job, not when her whole life had revolved around her mission. She hadn't given any thought to what would happen after she'd completed it, either.

You haven't thought about a lot of things, have you?

Ignoring the voice in her head, Flora concentrated on him. 'Such as?'

'There are a few positions vacant in the London office, and a couple of them would suit you very well, but…' He paused a moment. 'It wouldn't be a good look for me to appoint you without going through the proper procedures, especially considering you're my wife now.'

It didn't matter. She was closer to him as his wife, more than she'd ever have been as his PA.

'You're very rigid about your reputation,' she said without thinking. 'Why is that?'

His hand fell away abruptly, leaving her skin feeling cold. 'You must know why, Flora. Because of my father.'

She froze, watching his face. He'd never mentioned his father before, or his past. 'You mean, the investment scheme collapse?' she asked carefully.

'Yes.'

'It's been…what? Fifteen years? Surely you don't have anything left to prove now.'

'It doesn't matter how many years have passed. My name will always be linked to that scheme, and the misery it caused so many people.' His voice had flattened, all the warmth that had been in it leaching out. 'And, as such, my behaviour and that of my company will always be measured against what happened back then. I must be above reproach at all times, you know this.'

The lines of his face had hardened along with his voice, and inside her something hurt. It shouldn't, yet it did. Because looking at this caring, protective man now, it was becoming more and more difficult to see him as the man who'd ruined lives back then. The man she'd thought was ruthless and hard, manipulative, who merely paid lip-service to being a good employer and an upstanding businessman.

Except…she'd been wrong. She knew that now. He genuinely believed in all the good things he was doing— everything he'd done to protect her, for example—and certainly it was belief that shone in his eyes now.

'It must be hard,' she said impulsively. 'To feel that you have to be above reproach all the time.'

Something flickered in his gaze, as if he hadn't expected the statement. 'It's not…easy, no,' he admitted after a moment. 'But it's important to me that I set myself apart from my father. To do the right thing, be a better man than he was. I want the Constantinides name to be associated with helping people rather than destroying them.' There was a glow in his eyes now, fierce and hot, and for once it had nothing to do with sex. 'I will not be my father, Flora. I will never be him. I refuse.'

Apollo wasn't sure where his need to make Flora understand that he wasn't his father had come from. He'd spent his life setting himself apart from Stavros, and most people knew now that he was a completely different beast, and yet it felt very important that *she* know that.

Her opinion had never mattered to him before. She was his PA, she did what he told her, and he'd never thought beyond that. But somehow, at some point in the course of the past two weeks, her opinion had begun to matter.

She had begun to matter.

She was lying in his bed, a white sheet twined around her naked body, with her black hair in a tangle over her shoulders. Her eyes were the same dark grey as the thunder clouds outside, and she'd never looked more lovely.

Your wife.

A deep satisfaction stretched out inside him, that she was his.

Marrying her that day had been a very good decision indeed, especially when even the past two weeks of having her in his bed every night hadn't eased his hunger for her. In fact, if anything, having her constantly at his side had somehow made it even worse. Two weeks, and he was still just as obsessed with her as he'd been that first night.

Even right now, despite the fact that they had another event in a couple of hours, all he could think about was pushing her over onto her back and taking her mouth, hard and hot and hungry, then feasting on her body, making her scream, and then, and only then, thrusting into her, giving both of them the pleasure they craved.

It was madness. Somehow he'd gone from being in complete control of himself to being totally at the mercy of his need for Flora. Her and only her. No one else would do. No one else had managed to get under his skin so completely that it felt as if she'd always been there.

She'd released something in him, opened the door to the cage that some part of him had been trapped in, and she hadn't been ruined by it. No, if anything, he was the one who'd been ruined, and he couldn't bring himself to care.

Flora's clear grey eyes met his. 'You're not anything like him,' she said, as if she was well acquainted with Stavros and his foibles. 'You're not.'

This was a line of conversation he didn't particularly want to follow, but she'd told him the day they'd got married that she'd lost her parents. It hadn't been easy for her—he'd seen the grief in her eyes—so he could hardly shy away from telling her about his. Anyway, she'd have heard all about his father's infamous misdeeds. Many people had, especially after the suicide of one of the investors. Perhaps she had questions, and, if so, he had to give her the opportunity to ask them. He was her husband after all, and she should know what kind of man she'd married, even if the whole thing was a sham.

Not that he'd ever shied away from what his father had done or his own role in it. As he'd told her, he had his standards, and they were honesty and transparency at all times. He wasn't a hypocrite.

'You didn't know him,' he said bluntly. 'He used to tell me how like him I was, and there was a reason for that. I'd always wanted to be employed in the family business, follow in his footsteps, so when he said it was time for me to learn the ropes, I couldn't wait. I loved it.' He didn't look away, didn't bother to make the words sound better than they were. It was the pure, unvarnished truth and she should hear it. 'He wanted me to recruit as many people as I could into that damn scheme, so I did. I enjoyed it too, charming people out of their money. I believed it was for a good cause. A few things didn't add up, of course, but I ignored them, because I thought my father was a brilliant businessman, and he must have dealt with any discrepancies.' He paused a moment, then added, because he didn't want to sugarcoat it. 'I think deep down I knew the scheme was wrong somehow, but I loved my father and I wanted his approval. I wanted him to be proud of me.'

Flora's face had paled. Understandable really, considering what he was confessing. 'Apollo,' she began.

'No, let me finish. I hold myself to these standards because of what I did. Because I gave the worst parts of myself free rein. Charming people, convincing people to hand over their money, manipulating them… I loved all of it. But the pride Stavros took in what I'd done, I loved most of all.'

Flora said nothing, only looked at him.

'So now you know the truth,' he said into the heavy silence. 'I was complicit in my father's crimes, and that's why I have to set myself apart from them now. Why my reputation must be spotless. And why I can't ever lower my standards, not even once.'

A strange expression crossed her face then, one he couldn't read. 'You enjoyed it?' she echoed.

'Yes.' He didn't flinch away, didn't pretend it was something other than what it was. 'I liked the challenge. The rush I got when someone, who hadn't been interested, now suddenly was, because I'd convinced them.'

Her lashes fell, veiling her gaze, and she picked up the edge of the sheet, slowly pleating it with her fingers. She had tensed. 'So…when did you realise it was all a scam?'

He could remember it still, so clearly. First, a call from one of the investors, David Hunt, whom Apollo had brought on board personally, asking if there was any truth to the rumours that what Stavros was running was a Ponzi scheme. That had been news to Apollo, so he'd reassured Hunt that of course it was no such thing. Stavros would never do anything so terrible. A week later,

Hunt had killed himself, and subsequent enquiries into his financial dealings had revealed he'd invested everything in the Constantinides scheme.

The rumours got louder and the authorities got involved, and still Apollo had thought the whole thing was a media beat-up, defending Stavros to anyone who would listen. Then one day he'd come into the office to find his father in the process of shredding files. Stavros had thrust a pile at him and told him to destroy them, and it was in that instant he'd realised. That everything they'd been saying about Stavros was true. His father was a liar, a cheat, a fraud. His scheme had led to the death of someone, and he'd involved his own son in it.

Apollo had felt then as if the world had collapsed around him. He'd refused to shred the files, had demanded Stavros tell him why he'd done what he did, and Stavros had rounded on him in a fury, saying that Helios needed money and how else was he to get it? That if he truly loved this family, Apollo had to help get rid of the evidence, like his father had told him to.

Stavros hadn't cared that he'd stolen from people. He hadn't cared he'd led a man to his death. He hadn't even cared that he'd made Apollo complicit in the whole thing by lying to him about it. Apollo had been furious with his father, but had saved the worst of his fury for himself, for how he'd let his love for his father blind him to the truth.

He hadn't destroyed what remained of the evidence. He'd gone straight to the police with it and turned Stavros in.

After Stavros had gone to jail, his mother had refused

to speak to him, blaming him for not standing by his father when he'd needed him. The company collapsed into ruins, all their friends abandoned them, and he was left with nothing but blind fury and a crushing sense of guilt.

He'd had no way to deal with any of it, except to force it all down and do better. Remake the Constantinides name, get the business back on its feet. Make reparations to those who had lost money in the scheme's collapse, and then do everything he could to put as much good in the world as he was able.

So that's what he'd done, and what he continued to do.

'The first I heard was when one of the investors called and asked me if I knew anything about the rumours that my father was running a scam,' he said. 'I told him no, because I was sure my father would never do anything like that, but…' He didn't want to talk about this, not with his beautiful wife naked in his bed, not when there were other, far more pleasant things to be doing. But he forced himself to go on, because he'd promised himself all those years ago that he would be honest. 'A week later, the news came through that the man I'd spoken to had taken his own life. Subsequent investigations revealed that he'd sunk his life savings into my father's investment scheme, and that there were…irregularities.'

Flora nodded, but didn't look at him. Her fingers that had been pleating the fine linen of the sheet in a nervous movement had stilled. She seemed even more tense.

And why not? This was difficult to say, and probably worse to hear.

'The authorities wanted to investigate my father's

dealings,' he went on. 'And one day I came into the office to find him in the process of shredding files. I'd refused to believe the rumours that he was crooked, but that day… I realised they were all true. That a man had died because of him.' Apollo paused and the corrected himself, because he had to be honest. 'Because of me.'

Her hand closed convulsively on the sheet, bunching it up in her fist. Yes, this was a terrible thing he'd done. No wonder she'd gone so pale.

'Does it bother you?' he asked, after a moment, not knowing why it mattered to him, only that it did. 'My past? What my father did? What *I* did?'

'No,' she said.

But there was an edge in her voice that made him reach out and grip her chin, tilting her head back so he could look into her eyes. 'Flora,' he said softly. 'Don't lie to me. You know how I hate that.'

Shadows clouded her gaze, and there was a complicated expression on her face that he couldn't interpret. It looked as though she might speak, but then she leaned forward suddenly and her mouth was on his, kissing him hungrily.

There's something she's not telling you.

The thought occurred to him, clear as day, then her hands were on his shoulders, pushing him down onto the bed, and her mouth was tracking kisses down his neck, to his throat, over his chest, down to where he was hard and ready for her, as he always was.

Another thought occurred to him then, as her hot mouth closed around him, a belated thought, that she was trying to distract him. That what he'd told her *had* bothered her, but she hadn't wanted to admit it.

But then, as her tongue began to explore him, and her hands clasped him tight, in just the way he preferred, the thought went straight out of his head.

And there was nothing more but the exquisite pleasure of her mouth around him and the firm grip of her hands.

CHAPTER NINE

THEIR AFTERNOON INTERLUDE almost made them late to the party that evening, held in a rooftop bar in one of Kowloon's sky scrapers.

Flora—in a silvery, clinging cocktail dress that Apollo had bought for her, and her hair loose—tried to ignore the kernel of ice that sat in the pit of her stomach. Even the heat she and Apollo had generated in bed that afternoon hadn't managed to get rid of it.

She hadn't expected him to even mention his past, let alone talk about his own role in his father's scheme, or the moment he'd discovered that Stavros was a crook. Every word he'd said had been weighted down with regret, and it had been in his eyes too. The toll it had taken on him had been obvious, just as it had been obvious that he'd meant every word he'd said. He'd enjoyed deceiving all those people, her father included.

But he'd been deceived in turn. By Stavros. It had happened a long time ago, so he'd have been young, and like all young men he'd have wanted to prove himself to his father. And naturally, if he'd loved Stavros, then he'd have believed everything Stavros had told him.

It had all made sense to her.

She'd been a child when her father had died, and her mother had never gone into the details. She hadn't known that David had heard rumours surrounding the scheme, nor had she known that he'd called Apollo to ask if the rumours were true, or that Apollo had told her father everything was fine.

In the years after the scheme's collapse, Apollo had never made a secret of his own involvement in the scheme, or his regret for what had happened, but as she'd worked towards her goal of ruining him, she'd told herself that he must have been lying. That his regret and admissions of guilt weren't sincere, especially when he'd been given immunity for turning his father in.

Then, as she'd got to know him as a boss over the past year, his cold, brutally honest manner had seemed like dispassion, making her sure that he was only paying lip-service to feelings of guilt and regret. He didn't actually feel it. He didn't seem to feel anything at all.

Now though, after listening to him explain what had happened, she'd heard the pain in his voice. Heard the regret and the guilt, and, somewhere inside her, that icy effigy of him that she'd built up in her head, already undermined by the past two weeks of glorious passion, cracked right through.

Of course he cared. The man who held her in his arms every night, making her gasp and shudder and shake, wasn't some cold, unfeeling statue. He was honest, yes, but that honesty came from a genuine desire to tell the truth. To not lie to other people the way his father had lied to him.

And not only that, but he'd been affected deeply by the death of that investor he'd mentioned. An investor that could only have been her father.

She hadn't been able to look at him when he'd spoken about that, hadn't wanted to look into his eyes and see the truth, that the man she'd spent her life wanting to bring down had been as much a victim of his own father as hers had been.

Apollo had answered her questions with the same unflinching honesty that he answered any questions. Yes, he'd convinced her father to invest his money. Yes, he'd told David that there was nothing wrong, the scheme was totally legitimate.

Yes, he'd made a mistake and he regretted it. He blamed himself for it.

You were wrong about him. All this time you were wrong.

Flora's throat closed, tears prickling behind her eyes, no matter how hard she tried to blink them away. He was a good man, and she'd known it for a while now. Honest, protective, kind. He was everything the media said about him. More, he was also passionate, feeling things on a deep level. His heart was true.

Unlike yours.

The limo opened its doors into the sultry Kowloon evening, with the inevitable gathering of the press pack outside the skyscraper party venue.

Despite the humidity, Flora felt cold. She'd felt cold all

afternoon, the knowledge sitting inside her that it wasn't him who was the liar and the cheat, it was her. She was a con woman who'd taken in a good man, and not only was she lying to him, she was lying to herself.

Telling herself that it didn't matter if she lied to him. It didn't matter if he was hurt. That her parents deserved some kind of justice for how he'd ruined their lives.

Except he'd been ruined too, and by his own father.

How can you continue with your plan now? His heart has already been broken once, and you're intending to break it again.

Her throat closed, anguish collecting inside her. The thought of hurting him now felt like a knife in her side, and she knew all those doubts she'd had—that this plan had the potential to break her heart too—were true. It would.

In ruining him, she'd ruin herself.

The thunderstorm of the early afternoon had long gone, but the streets were still damp, neon staining the puddles everywhere. Cameras flashed and the press pack shouted questions as she and Apollo exited the limo.

He held out his arm to her and, even though she should have been used to seeing him in black tie by now, she was still caught by how devastatingly handsome he was. How her heart instinctively leaped whenever he turned his jungle green gaze on hers, glittering still with the remains of their afternoon passion.

This was the man she wanted to ruin. To cause him the same kind of pain that her father must have felt when he'd taken his own life. The same kind of hurt and betrayal she and her mother had experienced after David died.

She'd wanted to break him, yet now she knew the man behind that incredible gaze and list of accomplishments a mile long. The man who brought her coffee in the mornings and shielded her from the media, and who held her at night. The man who'd talked to her about everything under the sun, and who'd been nothing but honest with her...

She couldn't do it. She just couldn't.

She'd thought he was the villain all this time, but he wasn't.

The villain was her.

Flora clutched Apollo's hand as they walked up the steps to the building's entrance, tears filling her vision, her legs feeling unsteady. He glanced down at her with some concern, obviously spotting that she was in distress, which was a bad thing. He'd want to know what was upsetting her and, if he asked, she wasn't sure she'd be able to lie again.

She was so tired of lying.

What about justice for your parents' deaths?

But was it really justice to intentionally hurt someone? To cause them pain, simply because you yourself were hurting?

She knew the answer to that. It had been there all along, she just hadn't wanted to see it. Of course it wasn't justice. It was mean and petty and cruel. It was revenge, and there was nothing just about that.

Apollo had done what he could to mitigate his father's actions, and his own. He'd apologised and he'd paid out compensation. It wasn't his fault that her father had chosen the path that had caused the most pain. It wasn't his fault that her mother had refused that compensation in anger, before becoming ill with the cancer that would kill her.

None of that was Apollo's fault.

You need to tell him the truth then.

Yes, she did. Her mouth went dry at the thought of admitting that, for the entire year she'd been employed by him, she'd been hiding her background. That she'd planted those cameras. That his reputation was being called into question because of her. That she was the daughter of the man who'd killed himself...

She didn't know what he'd do when he found out the truth, but she did know one thing. He hated a liar. And there would be no more lazy afternoons in bed with his hands on her, making her feel beautiful and giving her pleasure. No more coffee in the morning, or little tasting plates. No more warm baths and him washing her hair.

No more of him at all.

He'd be furious with her, and he'd have every right to be.

As they reached the top of the steps, someone from the media pack yelled, 'What do you know about your secretary, Apollo? Do you have any comment to make about the rumours that she isn't who she says she is?'

Flora's blood turned to ice, and for a second she froze, completely unable to move. Apollo gave no sign of having heard the question, merely glancing at her, the concern in his eyes deepening.

Pull yourself together.

She gripped his arm, forced herself to give him a nod to indicate she was fine.

'Apollo!' The same person shouted again. 'Ask your wife about her background!'

Apollo's dark head turned in the direction of the media pack, and Flora wanted to tell him to keep moving, to go inside and get away from the questions, to find a quiet place where they could talk. But she didn't want to draw any more attention to herself than she already had.

'Flora!' someone else shouted, taking advantage of their pause at the top of the steps. 'Does your husband know about your family?'

Apollo's head whipped around in the other direction. Flora gripped his arm even tighter, feeling sick. 'Can we go inside?' she asked urgently. 'Please, I'm not feeling well.'

He glanced at her again, then nodded, ushering her into the building. The door slid closed, shutting out the clamour.

Inside was a vast marble foyer with lifts at one end, and Flora felt as if she was traversing a mountainside, her heels clicking on the floor and echoing in the silence.

Apollo said nothing as they came to a stop in front of the lift that would take them to the rooftop bar. A man in evening clothes waited outside the doors. He smiled and greeted them, then pushed a button, opening the lift doors and gesturing at them to step inside.

The ice inside Flora wouldn't go away as the doors slid shut.

The interior of the elevator was large and mirrored. She could see herself standing there in her glittering silver dress, Apollo tall and darkly beautiful standing beside her. Her face was pale, and there were dark circles under her eyes.

In the mirrored doors, she met his gaze, and felt her stomach drop away.

'Is there something that you're keeping from me, Flora?' he asked.

Her fingertips had gone cold, her heart beating hard and fast, but that didn't matter. What mattered was telling this man the truth she'd been hiding from him all this time.

He will hate you for it.

He would. And she would deserve that hate.

Her father had taken his own life for a reason, after all, and it hadn't just been because of the money. It couldn't have been. None of the other investors caught up in the scheme who'd lost everything had, so why had he?

You weren't enough for him. You never were.

The words whispered in her head as she looked helplessly back at Apollo, hoping desperately that the lift would finally stop, or maybe even plummet back down to the ground, and this terrible moment would end.

But neither of those things happened.

Say it. Tell him. Now.

He turned and his hands were heavy on her shoulders,

turning her to face him. There was concern in his eyes and worry, and she knew it was for her. Because he cared.

And in a sudden flash of insight, she suddenly understood why this moment was so hard, and why the thought of telling him made her feel physically sick.

Why, in the end, there was no other option for her but to give him the truth.

Because, despite all her justifications to herself about how this was only physical, that her heart wasn't involved, that she was perfectly in control, she wasn't.

She was in love with him and had been for the past two weeks, and if there was one thing this man deserved, it was the truth.

'Flora?' His eyes narrowed. 'Flora. Answer me.'

His grip on her was firm. There was no escaping his gaze.

No escaping this moment either.

She swallowed, her mouth bone dry, and made herself hold his gaze. She couldn't be a coward about this. He deserved the same honesty that he'd given her.

'Flora McIntyre is my legal name,' she said in an unsteady voice. 'But it's my mother's maiden name. My father was David Hunt. The man your father convinced to sink his life savings into that investment scheme. The man you told that the rumours were unfounded, and there was nothing to worry about.'

For a moment, Apollo just stared at her, as if he hadn't heard what she'd said. Then it must have penetrated, because his eyes widened in shock, and he dropped his hands from her shoulders, then took an unconscious step back, staring at her. 'What? What are you talking about?'

Flora forged on. 'Those statements the press were throwing at us… It's going to come out at some stage, but I hid my background from you. When I took the job at Helios, I didn't want you to know my history.'

He said nothing for a long moment, his expression still one of shock. Then, like water in a lake slowly freezing over, his expression hardened, his eyes becoming cold chips of dark green glass. 'And why would that be?'

Flora's fingers curled into fists. 'Because I've been planning to ruin you.'

Apollo couldn't move. Shock had frozen him where he stood. All he could do was stare at the woman in front of him, the same woman he'd married and had spent the last two weeks exploring every inch of. The woman who'd relaxed with him and laughed with him. Who'd unleashed her passion onto him every night and hadn't been afraid to have him do the same to her. Who was the only person he'd ever met who hadn't treated him either like a criminal or a paragon, but just as a man.

The woman who'd apparently been lying to him all this time and he hadn't known.

She'd been his PA for an entire year and had given no sign that she was anything but the woman he'd hired. Un-flappable, calm, serene. He'd known nothing about her, but at the time he hadn't thought he'd needed to. Then, when he realised he *did* want to know more about her, he'd thought he'd take it slowly, since she hadn't been very forthcoming with details about herself.

Except, there was a reason she hadn't been forthcoming.

If what she'd just said was true—if indeed he could believe anything she said—then she was David Hunt's daughter. The man who'd killed himself over the loss of his life savings. It had been years before Apollo had managed to get Helios into a position where he could give compensation to the victims. He'd located Hunt's family, but David's wife had refused any money, and nothing he'd been able to do had changed her mind.

It had been one of his life's biggest regrets.

Yet now, the daughter of that man was standing right in front of him, telling him she'd been lying about who she was all this time, and all because she wanted to ruin him. Lies of omission were still lies.

'Why?' He managed to dredge the word up somehow.

Flora had gone pale, yet her chin was held at a determined angle, and her grey eyes were clear. 'Because you ruined my parents' lives,' she said simply. 'So I was going to ruin yours.'

The shock echoed, ricocheting inside him and rebounding like a rock bouncing down a mountainside.

'How?' Apparently he'd been reduced to one-word questions.

'I wanted to get close to you,' she said. 'I spent a few years, actually, working towards getting hired by Helios, and then becoming your PA.' She swallowed then, the first sign of tension she'd shown, apart from her pallor.

'I was going to start with your reputation, and then I was going to ruin you financially, too.'

He stared at her, still trying to process what she'd said. 'You really thought you'd be able to ruin me?' he asked, because he couldn't get his head around it. 'By being my PA.'

'Yes.' Her voice was flat, as if she was having to force out the words, and he noticed that her hands were in tight fists at her sides. 'But then the photos came out and you offered to marry me instead of Violet, and… I decided financial ruin would affect too many other people, so I thought if I could get you to fall in love with me, then I could…hurt you. I could leave you, break your heart, the way my mother's and mine had broken.'

She used you the way your father used you, and you didn't see it. You only saw what you wanted to see, because you were obsessed with her. Just like you were obsessed with gaining your father's approval.

Something twisted inside him then, something else that had nothing to do with the present moment, and more to do with the past. A bitter grief, an endless guilt at what he'd done and the consequences that followed. But he shoved that aside, because the anger he felt about his own actions was a bottomless pit he couldn't afford to fall into.

Far better to be angry with her and her lies, at what she thought she could do to him, make him fall in love with her. As if he'd *ever* be so stupid.

Aren't you, though? You thought she was something she wasn't…

The rage inside him grew, at her for lying to him. For being so beautiful and passionate, and so accepting of him and his demands. For making his heart skip a beat every time he walked into a room. For smiling and laughing with him, for teasing and flirting with him. For being too good to be true.

And no matter how hard he tried to avoid it, he couldn't escape the fact that he was complicit in this too. For believing what she'd told him. For thinking that she was honest, that there was nothing manipulative about her. For baring parts of his soul to her, and not even realising that all this time, she must have hated him for it.

Yes, and for letting his heart take control when it should have been his brain. And he knew, deep down, that no matter what he told himself, it *had* been his heart that was involved, tthough how deeply, he didn't want to think about.

Because he should have been able to laugh this off. Fire her and put in place more stringent HR guidelines for Helios. Divorce her and send her away, never see her again, or take her to this event and pretend nothing had happened. Act as if it didn't matter.

Except he couldn't seem to find his usual cool veneer. His measured manner. There was only a blinding, hot rage, and a sense of deep betrayal.

'So all of this was a lie then?' he demanded, his voice much rougher than he wanted it to be. 'Every night we spent together, every time you called my name. That was all an act?'

Something flared in her eyes then, something that

looked like anguish. 'No,' she said hoarsely. 'No. None of that was a lie. That was all real, I promise.'

'Promise?' The word was acid on his tongue. 'How can you give me promises when you've been lying to me for months?'

'I know.' She swallowed yet again. 'I just didn't know—'

'Didn't know what?' His voice was as sharp as a whip-crack, and he didn't bother to temper it. 'That I hated liars? That I thought what we had together was something special, something different? That I thought *you* were different?'

She'd gone white. 'I didn't know you thought that. And I didn't know that you were everything people said you were.'

'So you thought that I was being insincere, did you? You thought that I was a liar, even though—' He bit the words off, swallowing them down. They were in a lift going to a party, and this was neither the time nor the place to have this confrontation.

Then he realised something else. She was the daughter of David Hunt, and once that came out, there would be interest in his past again, in the collapse of his father's scheme, in what had happened all those years ago. Tongues would wag, and he knew how it looked. He'd seduced the woman who'd been one of his father's victims—one of *his* victims…

There will be no divorce. Not yet at any rate.

Further down, beneath his anger, was something else, something that felt like pain, but he didn't want to acknowledge that. He didn't want to acknowledge anything at all except rage, and that he forced away, because he couldn't give into it, not here, not now.

'So,' he said finally into the heavy silence, 'I suppose I have you to thank for those photos?'

She was the colour of ash now, but he told himself he felt no sympathy. She'd brought this on herself. 'Yes,' she said faintly.

This time there was no shock, not even any surprise. Of course she'd engineered the photos. Of course. She was the reason he was now in this position. It was all her fault.

And you believed it, don't forget that. It was your idea to marry her.

Oh, he wouldn't forget. How could he? When the ring on her finger and the dress she wore was his?

'So this is revenge?' he asked.

She didn't flinch, and he would have admired her courage if he hadn't known that the only reason she was telling him all this now was because the press had somehow found out.

Another silence fell and still she didn't look away, her shoulders squared, as if bracing for a blow. 'I thought it was justice,' she said. 'What I told you in Paris was true. My father did die. He took his own life, and it broke my mother's heart, and mine. Mum didn't want the compensation you offered, she was too angry, so we had nothing. We had to sell the house, and then we were on the breadline. She had to work two jobs to keep us solvent, and then…' Her voice faltered. 'That's when she got sick. I lost her a couple of years ago.'

He'd felt sorry for her back in Paris when she'd told him about her parents. But he didn't feel sorry for her now. She'd had the opportunity to tell him the truth then, and she hadn't. She'd lied to him. She'd done exactly what his own father had done.

'My father went to jail,' he said, fighting to keep his voice level. 'My mother and I were left with nothing, also. Was that not justice enough?'

The look in her eyes flickered once again, darkening. 'You were the one who convinced him to sink all his money into that scheme. And you were the one who told him there was nothing to worry about.' She blinked, and he saw then that there were tears in her eyes. 'But that was before I…before you told me about…' She stopped.

Before tonight, he might have taken her in his arms and kissed away the tears. But it was tonight, and she'd dealt him a mortal blow. She'd hurt him knowingly, in the one place he was vulnerable, and he was too furious to care about her feelings.

Furious, and getting more and more so by the second.

The lift chimed, having reached the rooftop, but he put his hand on the button, keeping the doors closed. 'You worked for me for a year,' he snapped, unable to help himself. 'Did you not think, even for one moment, that I might have been a victim of my father, just as yours was? Did you really think that everything I've done to put right what he did wrong was a lie? That I didn't mean any of it?' His voice had risen, but he didn't try to quiet it.

Flora was still facing him, her chin high, but she was starting to tremble now and a tear had escaped one eye, slowly tracking down her cheek.

He was too angry to care about her tears. If she was hurt then good. She'd hurt him.

'I'm sorry,' she whispered. 'I was wrong.'

He didn't bother to ask himself why this mattered to him so much, why *she* mattered to him so much. He didn't bother to question why the sight of that tear made him feel an obscure kind of pain.

He only knew that he was angry, and there was an event they needed to get through, and none of what was happening between them could be allowed to show in public.

'It's too late for that,' he said coldly. Then he reached out and grabbed her hand, holding it tight within his.

She stiffened. 'What are you doing? You can't want me to go with you now.'

'No, I don't,' he said, brutally honest. 'But if your background comes out, what do you think people will say if I divorce you? If they think you seduced me, charmed me into believing you were who you said you were, I'll be a laughingstock. And if I get rid of you, I'll be the bastard who kicked one of the victims of my father's scam to the kerb. Either way, my reputation will suffer, so, yes. You'll have to come to the party with me, just as I'll have to pretend I knew who you were all along.'

He took his finger off the button and the doors slid open.

'Come,' he said brusquely. 'We have a party to go to.'

And he stepped out of the lift, into the noise and lights of the bar beyond.

CHAPTER TEN

FLORA FIERCELY BLINKED back the tears as he tugged her into the bar. Her heart hurt, everything hurt, but what he'd said in the lift made sense. She could plead a headache and go back to the apartment, but she was the one who'd created this mess. She was the one who'd lied to him, deceived him. Put at risk everything he'd worked for, and betrayed the growing understanding between them.

It was the least she could do to attend a bloody party, even if looking like she was enjoying herself was the hardest thing she'd ever done.

She couldn't believe he'd thought that everything that had happened between them in the past two weeks had been a lie. Surely he must know that it had been real. Surely… Then again, she could understand why he didn't. Everything else had been a total fabrication, so why wouldn't he think that?

Except her feelings for him weren't a lie. They were deeply and distressingly real, and they hurt. They hurt so much, because she had hurt him, and that was the worst part. A month ago, she'd believed all those untruths she'd told herself, believed the worst of him, based on nothing more than her own anger and pain. And in the space of a couple of weeks, everything had changed.

She'd fallen in love with the man she was supposed to hate, the man she was supposed to ruin, and what might have been the start of something wonderful was now in ashes, and she only had herself to blame.

She'd broken his trust, and he was never going to forgive her.

She was never going to forgive herself.

Before, whenever they'd arrived anywhere, he'd shortened his stride to match hers, but now he strode ahead without slowing, his hand still securely holding hers, leaving her to trot in order to keep up with him.

Her throat was tight and she wished with all her heart that she'd never decided on this little revenge plan of hers—and yes, it was revenge. Cold and petty and mean.

She didn't even feel a sense of relief that he knew about it now. No, all she could see was the flaring shock in his gaze and the look of betrayal that had crossed his face. Then the fury…

She'd come to love the distinct emerald glow in his eyes that was a sign of his passion. But the vivid emerald she'd seen in the lift had been nothing but rage.

Perhaps she should take some comfort in the fact that, if he'd been so furious, it must mean he felt something for her. But she wasn't comforted. All she knew was that she'd hurt him terribly, and she hated herself for it.

The bar had soaring ceilings and massive floor-to-ceiling windows, which gave magnificent views over the

city and the harbour. The decor was very minimalist, the
seating upholstered in black, the carpet too, with drama
and colour brought by gold light fittings.

A beautiful space, but Flora couldn't appreciate it. All
she was conscious of was Apollo's tall figure, tension
radiating from him, as he stopped by a small group of
people and glanced at her. His gaze couldn't have been
colder if he'd tried, but she forced a smile on her face
anyway. She would do this, she would bear it. It was the
least she could do for him.

Apollo introduced her to them, even as the names
sailed straight out of her head. All her attention was on
him, watching him talk, his green eyes glittering. He
was smiling, but she could see his rage. It was seething
in the air around them, making it difficult to breathe,
much less think.

She kept the smile plastered to her face, tried to act as
if nothing was wrong, but it was. Everything was wrong
and it was her fault.

*You're just like your father, giving out empty promises
you had no intention of keeping. Betraying the people
you care about because of your own pain. You're selfish, just like him.*

Something ached deep inside, something sharp and
edged, cutting away at the core of who she was, hurting, bleeding.

A woman she'd just been introduced to was looking
at her with some concern, and Flora knew she'd been
asked a question. But she couldn't remember what the

question had been, and she couldn't get any words out anyway, and now everyone was looking at her.

'You look very pale, dear,' the woman said. 'Are you quite all right?'

Flora could feel Apollo's gaze on her, the pressure of his anger pushing down on her, squeezing the life out of her, and abruptly she couldn't stand it anymore. She'd been pretending for too long, the course of her life directed towards a goal that had now been revealed to be a hollow, pyrrhic victory.

She'd wanted to ruin him, and yet all she'd done was ruin herself.

Flora wrenched her hand from his and turned, making her way blindly through the knots of people until she found the doors to the rooftop terrace. She pushed them open, and stepped outside, the humid air instantly wrapping itself around her.

The massive city stretched out below her, the glittering neon turning Hong Kong into some kind of science fiction fantasy.

There was no one else on the terrace, so she stood there for a time, looking over the magnificent view of the city and the bay, struggling not to let the tears fall, feeling as though someone had ripped a hole in her chest.

'Flora.'

His voice came from behind her, deep, rough, and she turned around sharply, swiping a hand across her cheek to make sure there were no tears. She didn't want him to see how awful she felt. It was her problem to deal with. She didn't want to make it his.

His face betrayed nothing, his gaze level and flat. 'What are you doing out here? We need to show a united front, remember?'

'Yes,' she said, trying to keep her tone as even as his. 'Of course. I just…needed some air.'

His cold green gaze swept over her, studying her as if she was a stranger, which was of course what she was to him now. 'Why are you upset? You were the one who put us in this distasteful situation. Deal with it.'

His voice was like ice, and her heart ached for the warmth and the heat that she'd had for the past two weeks. The little displays of care and concern that had made her feel so good, the desire in his eyes that had made her feel beautiful.

You don't deserve any of it. You never have.

No, she didn't, she understood that now. And he didn't either. He didn't deserve what she'd done to him, and that whispered apology in the lift hadn't been nearly enough.

She turned to face him. 'I'm sorry,' she said starkly. 'I'm sorry I lied. I'm sorry I put you in this situation. I should have known the kind of man you were when I first started working with you, but… I didn't. I shouldn't have done it, but…'

He said nothing.

She took a breath, and went on, wanting him to understand that the problems were hers, not his. 'I loved my father. I loved him so much, and he always promised that he'd take care of Mum and me. That we were the most important things in his life. And then…he left us. He broke all those promises he made, and left Mum and me with nothing, nothing at all. She had to go out and work two jobs just to keep a roof over our heads. And then…it was six years after Dad died that she got cancer. I don't know if it was the stress or what, but… It was incurable.' Her throat was tight and she had to swallow to even breathe. 'When she died, I was all alone.' Somehow there were tears on her cheeks, even though she hadn't known she was crying, but she didn't bother to wipe them away. 'After they were gone, I had nothing and no one, and I was just…so angry. Angry at Dad for leaving us the way he did, for not even thinking about the effect it would have on us. But he was gone, and you and your father weren't, so… I blamed you instead.' She stopped, her throat aching. What was the point of telling him this? Why would he care? It was justification after justification, and she knew it. 'I'm sorry, Apollo. I didn't know what kind of man you were until…'

He took a step towards her, the lines of his beautiful face hard. 'You think I care about any of that? When you lied to me? When you put me in a situation where I had to go against *everything* I believed in, and lie too? After I've made my entire life about transparency and honesty.' He took another step. 'You made me a liar, Flora. You duped me, the way my father did, then you turned me into a liar like him.'

Rain had begun to fall again, a sudden and thick tropical downpour.

Flora ignored it as her dress soaked through, his words like stones being thrown at her, causing an abrupt protective anger to flicker to life.

He had a right to his anger, but there were some choices he'd made that had turned the whole situation into something more complicated than it had needed to be.

She took a step towards him, the rain making her dress stick to her skin. 'You didn't have to lie,' she shot back. 'This marriage was your idea in the first place. There were other things you could have done. It didn't have to involve—'

'You?' He was standing right in front of her, as soaked to the skin as she was, his emerald eyes blazing. '*You* involved me, Flora! You put at risk everything I worked for. Everything I—'

'You destroyed my family!' She shouted, uncaring who heard, all the pain and rage overflowing inside her. 'My father *died* and so did my mother, and I was left all alone. Dad didn't care what would happen to us after he was gone and, as for Mum, I was nothing but a mill-stone around her neck that she didn't need!' She kept on shouting, the hurt demanding some kind of outlet. 'I lost everyone I loved and everyone who loved me, and all because of you!'

Apollo was so close, staring down at her, the look in his eyes electric, blazing. 'Don't act as if this was something you were forced into, Flora,' he bit out. 'It's all about choices. Your parents had choices, and if you didn't like them, that's got nothing to do with me!'

His tall figure was wavering in front of her, and she wasn't sure if it was due to the tears in her eyes or the rain. Even now, even like this, hurling yet more painful truths at her, he was the most beautiful man she'd ever seen.

She took an unsteady breath. 'I know,' she said, in a voice thick with tears. 'I know. I believed him. I thought he'd take care of us, that he'd never let anything bad happen to us, but I was wrong. I was wrong about *everything*.' She swiped her hand over her face again and turned away, not wanting him to witness the breaking of her heart, but then a firm hand gripped her shoulder and she was pulled around to face him again.

He was breathing fast, the lines of his face taut. Then he glanced up at the sky, muttered a curse, grabbed her hand in an iron grip and strode towards the doors, pulling her inside.

Unable to break his grip, Flora had no choice but to run behind him to keep up. He shouldered through groups of people, apparently not caring that they were soaking wet and everyone was staring at them.

He led her down a short hallway, before finding a door and opening it, dragging her inside and kicking the door shut behind them.

It was a small powder room, with a couch and an armchair, and a mirror above a little vanity along one wall, not that Flora was taking much notice.

She was soaking wet and shaking with emotion. Fury and guilt and a pain so sharp and raw it felt as if someone had taken a scalpel to her soul. She opened her mouth, to say what she didn't know, but then Apollo was reaching for her, gripping her shoulders and pushing her against the wall.

His hair was soaked, licking across his forehead like black flames, his eyes a dark blazing emerald. Her heart kept tripping over itself just looking at him.

The grip he had on her verged on painful, every inch of his magnificent, powerful body tense with fury. 'I don't care what you lost,' he said through gritted teeth, his Greek accent becoming pronounced. 'I was only trying to protect you, that's all I was ever trying to do with this farce of a marriage. And as for breaking my heart… You'd never be able to do that, not in a million years. How could I ever love a woman who lied to me?'

She was shivering now, but it wasn't because she was cold. Not even with her wet dress plastered to her and the air con in the room. No, it was because of him, because the heat of his body was radiating into her like a vast, dark fire, and all she could think was how had it come to this?

He'd been the target of her anger for so long and she'd told herself she hated him. Except she didn't, it was the opposite, and now the tables had been turned. She was now the object of his anger, his hate, and the thought that she'd broken his trust so selfishly made her feel like the worst person in the entire world.

She wanted to say something, offer another apology, but he saved her from answering by bending his head, his mouth suddenly on hers, and it felt as if the very air around them caught fire, ignited by the heat of their connection.

It was a raw kiss, fuelled by rage and pain, guilt and hunger.

He bit her bottom lip hard, making her gasp, and then she was kissing him back, trying to bite him the way he was biting her, draw blood, take out this aching swell of emotion on him in some way. But he wouldn't let her.

He grabbed her wrists and forced them down to her sides. 'I can't divorce you,' he said low and rough. 'No matter how much I want to. We have to stay married for six months to a year in order for the blowback about your background to die down. But now you owe me, Flora. For all the months you lied to me, and for those ill-advised photos. For the trust you betrayed. Do you understand?'

She was breathing very fast, her mouth full and sensitive, her whole body wanting him desperately. She wished she could tell him that he was wrong, she didn't owe him, but she couldn't. She couldn't lie any more.

'Yes, I understand,' she said hoarsely, because what else could she say?

'So here is how our marriage is going to be.' He gripped her wrists tighter. 'I want something in return, and that will be you, in my bed every night, because as much as I don't want to want you, I do. You will act on the outside as if you've never been happier than to be in my presence. You will give me anything I want whenever I ask, and you will not refuse.'

She swallowed. 'Why?'

'Because I never gave you any reason to doubt me, and yet you did, this whole time. So this will be your apology. You will give your trust to me without receiving anything in return.'

'And if I don't want to?'

'Then leave. I won't stop you. But you will never see me again if you do.'

Flora knew she should take the escape he offered, run away and never see him again, that it would be kinder to both of them if she did. But she couldn't, she already knew that. The thought of leaving him was even more unbearable than the thought of staying with him.

'Okay,' she said hoarsely.

'Your agreement,' he bit out. 'Say it.'

'Yes, I agree. To everything.'

The look in his eyes flared. 'Now, I want you. And you will let me do anything I want to you, right here, right now.' There was a cruel twist to his mouth. 'But you will get no satisfaction from it, understand? If you come before I say so, you will be punished.'

A quiver ran the length of her body. The tattered remnants of her pride wanted to push him away and walk out, but it was too late for that, far too late. All she could feel was his heat, the smell of rain and his aftershave were making her dry-mouthed with desire. He still wanted her, that was something, and so she would give herself to him. She couldn't do anything else.

She would give him anything and everything.

She stood there as he dropped to his knees in front of her, pushing her wet dress up to her hips, before grabbing the fine lace of her underwear and ripping it away. She was trembling by then, her knees weak, the ache between her thighs almost as needy and raw as the ache in her heart.

He looked up at her, his gaze fierce. 'You will not

touch me. That, you'll have to earn.' Then, without waiting for her to speak, he put his hands on her thighs and gripped them, then used his thumbs to delicately spread the soft folds of her sex. Then he leaned forward and covered it with his mouth.

A raw bolt of electric pleasure lanced through her, making her gasp as his tongue began to explore. She'd learned over the past couple of weeks that he was extremely good at this, and now he used his knowledge of her to devastating effect. Licking, teasing, stroking her so that her knees became so weak only his hands on her thighs were holding her up.

It was all she could not to grab his shoulders or thread her fingers through his hair, touch him the way she was desperate to, but he'd forbidden her. She didn't have to do what he said, she knew that, but he'd made it impossible for her to do otherwise.

She *did* owe him.

She loved him and she'd broken his trust, and now all she wanted to do was make it up to him.

He did something with his tongue then that made her shake like a leaf, and she had to put her hands over her mouth to stop the cries. She tried to think unsexy thoughts, anything to stop the relentless drag of pleasure, but nothing seemed to work. She wanted to prove to him that she didn't doubt him by doing what he asked and hold back her orgasm, but she didn't think she could. And then his tongue sank deep inside her and she closed her eyes, screaming against her own hands as pleasure exploded around her and she was lost to it.

* * *

Apollo felt her tremble, heard her hoarse, muffled scream, tasted the flavour of her orgasm as she came, so sweet it pierced his soul. He didn't understand that sweetness, didn't know why it still had that effect on him, even knowing now what she'd done to him.

He was still furious, too. As furious as he'd been the moment she'd lifted her chin and told him that she'd been lying to him. That she was nothing but a con woman and a charlatan, just like his father.

Perhaps that's why he was so angry. Because of what Stavros had done to him all those years ago, duping him the way Flora had duped him. Perhaps the sense of betrayal had nothing to do with her specifically, but was only an echo of that long-ago breach of trust his father had committed. Because yes, he'd trusted her—he'd had no reason not to—and she'd broken that trust.

He shouldn't be here now with her. He should have continued walking through the party, pulling her along behind him. They could have left via the back way, out of the bar, without anyone being the wiser, then gone back to his apartment where he would have left her in the bedroom alone.

He hadn't needed to drag her into this room. He hadn't needed to tell her exactly how their marriage would proceed from now on. All he'd needed, to continue this farce, was her presence in public, not in private.

Yet, as he'd stood on the outside terrace in the pouring rain, watching her eyes go silver with fury as she'd told him about her anger, about how she'd lost everyone she'd ever loved and that he was to blame, all he could think about was how much he wanted her, even now, even after what she'd done.

Beneath his own anger, there had been the ghost of something softer, something that had ached for the pain he'd seen in her eyes, but he'd ignored it. He hadn't wanted to feel sorry for her. He'd tried hard to hold on to his control then, but even standing amid the shards of his broken trust in her, somehow she managed to get under his skin. She'd been standing there in the rain with her wet dress plastered to her, the neon skyline making her look as if she'd been dipped in molten silver.

She was so beautiful, and all his fury, looking for an outlet, had been alchemised full force into breath-stealing desire before he'd even been aware of it.

All that seemed to matter was having her, pouring out his rage into her willing body, punishing her for what she'd done to him by giving her pleasure but no release. It would all be on his terms now, not hers. She'd given up the right to that when she'd forced him into this lie of a marriage.

'You didn't have to lie...'

The words she'd flung at him on the terrace outside, about the choices he'd made himself, echoed in his head, but he ignored them. He was too angry with her to accept his own culpability in this mess, and now he was too hard to think about anything but having her.

She was shaking as he rose to his feet. He didn't touch her, didn't bother to adjust her dress. Instead, he reached into his pocket, got out his wallet and found a condom.

'You disobeyed me.' He'd planned to sound cold and brusque, but his voice came out hot and rough instead. 'You came when I told you not to, which means you don't deserve to have anything more. This is for me, Flora. Just for me.'

She didn't move as he ripped open the condom packet, then unzipped his trousers. Her eyes darkened even further as he dealt with the protection before stepping closer to her. He slid a hand down the back of her thigh and behind her knee, then he hauled her leg up and over his hip, spreading her open. She gasped softly, arching back against the wall, damp black hair tangled over her shoulders.

'Do you hear me?' He positioned himself before thrusting hard and deep, pinning her. 'It's my turn.'

'Yes,' she whispered on a gasp. 'Oh...yes...'

He pushed deeper, holding her pressed to the wall, grey eyes gone ever darker, nearly black, staring into his as if he'd mesmerised her. 'Why you?' The words escaped before he could stop them. 'Why can I not stop thinking about you? Why can I not stop wanting you?'

She shuddered as he began to move, a deep insistent rhythm that made her arch and her mouth open, soft panting breaths escaping. 'I...have hated you,' she said softly. 'I hated you so much, and yet...it changed. I didn't know...that it would.'

Pleasure had him in a vice, even as he felt her inner muscles tighten around him, holding him, giving him the most exquisite friction. 'This could have been something.' He slid the strap of her dress roughly down, uncovering one beautiful breast. '*We* could have been something, Flora. But you ruined it.'

A shiver rocked her as he toyed with her nipple—her lashes lowering, her pallor gone, washed away by the flush of pleasure staining her skin. 'I'm sorry,' she whispered. 'I'm so selfish. I hurt…the people I love.'

Through the building heat, he could hear the note of pain in her voice.

'Look at me.' He pinched her nipple hard, making her lashes lift abruptly, her gaze coming automatically to his, and he could see the same pain in her eyes too. 'What are you talking about?'

She swallowed, her breath coming harder, faster. Watching him as he moved inside her. Her eyes were reddened and a tear slid slowly down her cheek. 'I… l-love you, Apollo, and I hurt you. And you will never know how sorry I am for that.'

The strangest bolt of electricity went through him then, part pure physical pleasure, part a surge of what felt like joy, and over the top, another flare of anger. Because why tell him this now? After she'd conned him. Broken his trust and betrayed him.

'Liar,' he ground out. 'How will I ever know if you're telling the truth?'

'I told you,' she murmured, another tear sliding down her cheek. 'The past two weeks…it was all real. My feelings for you are real too.' Her eyes were wide and dark, and he thought she was telling the truth, but again, how would he know?

Now wasn't the time for this discussion, though, so he

didn't speak. Instead, he leaned forward and licked her tear away, then covered her mouth with his.

He kissed her with raw passion, and a savagery he hadn't thought was in him, pouring all his anger out and into her, and she didn't pull away, didn't protest. She didn't touch him either, as he'd told her, only moved with him.

He wanted to take his pleasure first, to leave her hungry and wanting and desperate, but even in the depths of his rage, he couldn't quite bring himself to do that. So, as the orgasm began to take him, he slid a finger between her legs, down to where they were joined, and felt her body convulse around his, a cry of release escaping her.

Then he was moving harder, faster, until the rising pleasure blinded him, swamping him utterly.

Afterwards, he leaned against the wall, crushing her against it, her body soft and warm despite the fact that they were both damp from the rain. She felt small and fragile, and she was shivering, and the protector in him wanted to gather her up and hold her close, to soothe her somehow.

He crushed the urge.

She's still your wife, though. There's no point in being needlessly cruel.

He'd never been a cruel man, and he wouldn't be cruel now. But things wouldn't go back to the way they were before all of this had happened either. He'd given her the new terms of their marriage, and had offered her a way out, and she hadn't taken it. Which meant this was their marriage now. He still wanted her, and he'd be damned if he was going to spend six months to a year being celibate, but she'd get nothing else from him.

She'd betrayed him. The same kind of betrayal he'd felt when he'd walked into the office that day and found his father shredding documents, and realised that the man he respected and loved had been lying to him. Had charmed him and manipulated him into doing the most terrible things, and all for his own gain.

Flora was just like that. Charming him, manipulating him, causing him to go against everything he believed in, and all because she was angry.

He couldn't forgive it, as he'd already told her. And he never would.

Pushing himself away from her, he dealt with the condom and adjusted his clothing. Then he turned back to her and, without a word, helped her cover herself. Her hands were shaking as she drew the strap of her dress back over her breast, and again he had to crush the part of him that wanted to hold her.

Instead he held out his hand. 'The party is waiting for us.'

She pushed her hair back and glanced at the door, then back at him. 'You can't mean to go back to it. After that?'

'Yes. As I've already said, it's even more important we look as if we're together and madly in love now, especially with your identity in question.'

She blinked, her eyes dark. Some of her mascara was running and her mouth looked red and full, as if she'd bitten it. 'But my dress…your suit…'

'We'll tell them we got caught in the rain, which we did. That at least I don't have to lie about.'

She flushed. 'I'm not wearing underwear.'

'You can go without.' He held out his hand more insistently. 'It will make it easier to avail myself of you later.'

She took his hand, which felt small in his. 'I...don't think I can do this.'

He tightened his grip and gave her a feral smile. 'You've managed to deceive everyone beautifully until tonight. Just keep doing that.'

Her father took his own life and she lost everything, don't forget. That's what she said.

Yes, he remembered. But he was in no mood to hear about her past or her reasons for lying to him. His well of sympathy had run completely dry.

Flora had no answer to that, so he turned and pulled open the door, stalking back into the party.

It was a nightmare, the way that first party they'd gone to had been a nightmare. Of her, in her damp dress, with her black hair in a tangle, her mascara running and her mouth still full and red from his kisses. Knowing he'd ripped her underwear away and she wasn't wearing anything underneath. Of still wanting her despite everything.

He smiled at people, made light of their damp clothes, pretended he was still as in love with Flora as ever, yet it had never felt more like an act. He'd never felt the toxic combination of rage and desire more strongly than he did right now.

They moved through the crowd, Flora barely saying anything, the smile on her face more a rictus than anything else, and he didn't want to feel sorry for her. God, he'd even told her all about his betrayal that afternoon in bed. About how he'd found out what his father had done, and what he'd done after it. He'd talked about her father's suicide too, and how that had affected him.

He'd bared a part of himself to her and her response hadn't been to tell him the truth, but to distract him with sex. Well, that was fine. She'd get nothing but sex from him now.

He made them stay another two interminable hours before he finally called the car to take them back to his apartment.

He'd been planning to have her as soon as they got home, but one look into her silvery eyes told him that she was expecting it, that she wanted him just as much as he wanted her.

Too bad. He didn't want to give her what she wanted.

'Go to bed,' he said brusquely. 'I'm too angry for anything more tonight.'

Then he turned on his heel, strode down the hall to his study and shut the door behind him.

CHAPTER ELEVEN

FLORA SAT IN the shade of the bougainvillea, on the terrace of Apollo's beautiful Greek villa. It had been built high on a hill above a little fishing village with the sea stretched out below her, a swathe of measureless aching blue.

They'd arrived from Hong Kong a couple of days before, and while the villa itself and the surroundings were heart-wrenchingly beautiful, Flora hadn't been able to appreciate any of it.

Apollo had withdrawn from her completely. It was as if he was a stunning island that she desperately wanted to visit, yet had no way to cross the vast gulf of the ocean between them.

The only attention he paid her was at night, in his bed, where he turned from ice into flame in a matter of seconds, drawing pleasure from her again and again. As she'd promised, she denied him nothing. She'd thought he might do as he'd vowed back in Hong Kong, leave her desperate and wanting, without any satisfaction, but he didn't. He'd never been a selfish lover and he still wasn't, not even in the depths of his fury.

In a couple of days they were supposed to be giving interviews about their great love affair and marriage, and there was to be a photoshoot too, and she was dreading it. Yes, she'd spent a year pretending to be someone she wasn't as his PA, but the thought of pretending there was nothing wrong between her and her husband made her feel exhausted.

Her husband. Was he even that now? Apart from the sex, he ignored her even more than he had as her boss.

Regardless, she didn't want to keep pretending, keep lying. That's why she'd told him she loved him back in Hong Kong. Maybe that had been a mistake—he'd certainly looked anything but happy at the declaration—but she'd wanted to be honest with him. She couldn't bear the thought of lying to him yet again.

But you'll have to keep lying.

That was true. The rumours about her background had been swirling since that night in Hong Kong. And so, to keep ahead of any misinformation, Apollo had issued a statement saying that he'd known all about Flora's family history right from the first, and he'd been keeping quiet about it to protect her. Of course he knew that she was David Hunt's daughter, but that hadn't factored into their marriage.

He hadn't run the statement by her first, he'd simply issued it without her approval, but she didn't protest. How could she? She'd keep lying to the public, pretending she was deliriously happy, just as he did, but she would not lie directly to him. Never to him. Never again.

There were yachts out in the bay, scudding across the

waves, and the air was full of the smell of salt and dry earth, and the spice of some nearby flower.

She wished she could enjoy it, but her heart hurt too much. What she wanted, now that the initial shock of her deception had passed, was to tell him everything. Not for the sake of unburdening herself, but so he had some context at least. Then she wanted him to tell her about his past, about his father, about how he blamed himself for her father's death, because he did. She knew he did.

Of course, whether he told her anything at all was up to him, she had no right to ask, and she had no right to ask him to listen to her, either. But still. She wanted it.

After that, well. She didn't know. They'd have to stay married, but did he still want her to move in with him when they got back to London? If so, he hadn't said.

She didn't have to stay in Greece. She could leave, go back to London on her own, try and pick up the remains of her life somehow, but… That would leave him having to clean up the mess of their marriage and she couldn't do that. And as for the remains of her life… What even was that? She'd spent years aiming for this one goal, the complete ruination of Apollo Constantinides. and she'd cut out everything that hadn't directly related to that goal. And now, as she wasn't pursuing it any more, what was there left for her? An empty bedsit and an empty, directionless life.

Isn't that what you deserve?

Probably. She'd made him feel like he was his father, that's what he'd hurled at her that terrible night in Hong Kong. She'd taken him in, duped him, just as his father had, turning him into something he hated. a liar. So, yes, she did deserve it.

She'd hurt him where he was most vulnerable, and when she should have told him the truth, that afternoon when he'd bared some of his soul to her, she hadn't.

Now, though, every night in his arms, she bared her soul to him, trying to show him what he meant to her. Without words, because at least her body had never lied, but whether he understood that or not, she didn't know. He didn't speak at night and, in the mornings, she always woke up alone.

Her heart ached as she glanced along the stone terrace towards the white villa. The dark wood-framed doors were steadfastly shut, as they had been the few days she'd been here, even though she kept hoping he would push them open and come and join her. But he hadn't.

Maybe you should be the one to go to him.

The vice around her heart tightened. She could, but he might not want to see her. He might not want to listen to her, and then what would she do? All the people she'd ever loved had left her. First her father, by making a choice she was still furious about all these years later. and then her mother. Cancer hadn't been a choice, but her mother hadn't fought it. She'd succumbed quickly, as if she had no heart to keep on living.

No one wants to stay for you.

Her throat closed, more stupid tears were wavering behind her eyes. No, no one had. And the one man who might have, had she not ruined it the way he'd said back in Hong Kong, had cut himself off from her.

So what? Yes, life dealt you a crappy hand, but that's all you'll ever have if you don't go out and fight for him. You had the determination to ruin him, now find that same determination and love him.

A small electric shock bolted through her, stealing her breath.

It was true. that stubborn determination to follow her goal had led her to his point, and nothing had really changed except the goal itself.

She loved him. She wanted him. She wanted this marriage to be real, but if she was going to make that happen, she couldn't sit here wallowing in self-loathing. She couldn't keep obsessing over her losses and miring herself in fury.

There was no way to change the past, what had happened, had happened. But she had the power to change her future.

To let go of her anger and choose love instead.

She had to go to him, talk to him. Tell him what she wanted, which was to spend the rest of her life making it up to him, because a life loving him was better than a life alone, with nothing but her rage to comfort her. And if he didn't want that then...well, she'd have to deal with it.

Flora let out a breath, and with it she finally let go of the anger that had been fuelling her for years, the anger at her father's choices and the unfairness of life that had taken her mother too, burning like a flame in her heart. Yet the flame didn't flicker and go out. It began to burn. Brighter, more intensely, as a far more powerful feeling took its place.

It was sweeter and it ached, but it was right. It was true. It was love.

Flora pushed herself from the chair and walked across the terrace to the doors. Inside was the cool stone of the floor of the living room and its heavy-beamed ceilings, with lots of couches and low armchairs all upholstered in white linen.

Apollo would be in his office, so she went down the hallway, pausing outside the door to take another breath to calm her nerves, before pushing it open.

It was empty though.

She searched the entire house without finding him, only to hear the sound of splashing coming from the pool on the other side of the house.

The pool area was built into the side of a cliff, with an infinity pool overlooking the sea, and a white stone terrace scattered with sun loungers.

Flora came out through the doors, stepping onto the warm white stone.

In the pool in front of her, one powerful olive-skinned arm rose and fell, as Apollo pulled himself through the water.

She stood for a moment, her heart full and aching in the cage of her ribs, watching him. He was graceful in the water, and strong, sleek as a shark.

Eventually, gathering her courage, Flora walked over to the edge of the pool and waited for him to notice her. He did another couple of laps before finally lifting his head from the water, raising his hands to push his wet hair back from his face. His green eyes were cold, no hint of welcome in them.

Flora's mouth went dry, a combination of nerves and appreciation at how the water sheened his skin, emphasising every hard, cut muscle of his chest and abdomen.

'Yes?' he inquired imperiously. 'What do you want?'

She swallowed. 'Can I talk to you, please?'

'I'm swimming.'

'I know.' She held his gaze, willing him to soften, even just a little. 'But this is important.'

He said nothing for a moment. Then he put his hands on the side of the pool and pushed himself out, in a demonstration of effortless strength. The water streamed off his magnificent body, making him look more like Poseidon than Apollo, and the ache in her heart deepened.

How to measure her love for this man? How to encompass his beauty? Words weren't enough and they never would be. Yet words were all she had.

He strode to one of the sun loungers and picked up the towel lying on it, then began to dry himself off. 'Make it quick,' he said curtly. 'I have things to do.'

Flora steeled herself. She had no idea what he felt for her, if he even felt anything at all after Hong Kong. But she knew what she felt. That was real and she had to trust it. She had to trust herself and her love for him.

She had to cross the gulf between them, because if she didn't try, she knew she'd regret it for the rest of her life.

'Apollo,' she said, as he wrapped the towel around his lean hips and stared at her. 'What I said back in Hong Kong was true. I'm in love with you.'

If the words made an impression on him, he didn't show it. 'And?'

Maybe he doesn't care.

He sounded so cold that it might very well be true. But then, if he didn't care, why was he still so angry? A person only got really mad if they cared a great deal, didn't they?

'You're angry still.' She had to fight to hold his gaze.

His mouth was a hard line. 'Yes,' he said flatly. 'I am.'

Well, that was the one thing she could count on with him, at least. He was honest. He'd never lied to her.

'I can apologise again if you like,' she went on determinedly. 'I can apologise as many times as necessary.'

'The first time was already more than enough.'

'And yet you're still angry.'

'Did you really expect my feelings to change just like that? Because you offered me an apology?' There was a distinct icy glitter in his eyes. 'I told you that I won't forgive you. I meant it.'

Was there really no way for her to bridge this space between them? Was there really no way back to him? She had try. She'd come this far.

Flora took a soft, silent breath. 'My dad loved Mum and me, but he was never good with money. He was always into these get-rich-quick schemes, and Mum loved him so much she was blind to his faults. When he told her what he was doing, that the returns were too good not to invest everything, she supported him. He wanted to better our lives, to take care of us, that's what he promised. Then he just…betrayed that promise. He betrayed us. He…didn't care enough about us to stay, to help us through the devastation. He took the easy way out.' She didn't bother to hide her bitterness. She was going to be nothing but honest from now on. 'So, I told you that we had to sell the house, and Mum had to get two jobs. It was all she could do to earn enough to keep our heads above water. I kept thinking how much easier it would be for her if she didn't have me.'

Apollo didn't say anything, but he didn't move either, the expression on his face impassive.

'She had no time for me,' Flora went on, clasping her hands together to stop them from shaking. 'She had no time for anything except work. I was in high school when she got sick. It was cancer, and I think she just gave up, because it was quick in the end. But I was so angry about it. I think… I was really angry at her for refusing the compensation money, and that if we'd had it, she wouldn't have worked so hard and got sick. But being angry at her was unfair, and I felt it so very deeply, I had to have some outlet and so… I blamed Dad.' Somehow she'd lost a little of her courage, so she turned to stare across at the ocean, since that was easier than looking at the stony expression on Apollo's face. 'I had no one after she died, only this anger at the unfairness of it all. Dad was gone, I couldn't direct it at him, and I just felt… powerless. Eventually, I found myself reading everything about the collapse of your father's scheme, about all the people involved. I saw that you'd been the one who'd convinced Dad to invest all his money. And I read that you'd turned your father in and escaped prosecution.'

The breeze lifted her hair on her shoulders and she wanted to turn around, to see if he was still there, still listening, but she didn't. This was all the olive branch she could offer him and, if he refused to take it, that was his prerogative. 'Your father had died in jail, so I couldn't touch him anymore. But I could get to you. I could make you pay for what happened to my family, and so that's what I set out to do.' She watched a boat zigzag across the blue water. 'I told myself it was justice, but it wasn't. I was just so blinded by anger in the end. So sure of the truth. That you were a liar, a master manipulator. I was sure that you were only paying lip-service to all those good deeds you did, that your bluntness was coldness, ruthlessness. That you didn't care.' Had he gone? Was she only talking to thin air?

'I wanted you, though,' she forced herself to go on. 'Even then, even when I told myself I hated you, I wanted you so badly. And then…' Her voice cracked. 'That two weeks we spent together was the happiest of my life. I didn't know who you really were until then, and I didn't realise that I'd been lying to myself. I wanted to believe that you were a terrible person so badly, because the only alternative was admitting that I was the terrible one. That I wasn't important enough for my father to make a different choice, and my mother not to fight her illness.'

Apollo stared at Flora's still figure. She wore a loose, tiered dress of white linen, held up by ties on each of her shoulders, and her black hair lay glossy and thick down her back.

He wanted to be angry with her. He wanted to turn his back on her and walk away. The past week since Hong Kong had been so difficult, even though he'd tried not to let it be. He thought pouring all of his anger and betrayal into her more-than-willing body every night in bed would help. He'd even told himself that he'd leave her wanting and unsatisfied, in punishment for what she'd done to him, but when the time came, he could never do it.

In bed, undone and abandoned in his arms, was the only time he knew she was honest with him, and the orgasms he wrung from her were always real. There was nothing fake about her response to him, and so he could never stop from proving that to himself.

Her background had come out now, and, as he'd thought, the media had driven itself into a frenzy over how he'd married the daughter of David Hunt, the victim of his father's scheme, who'd killed himself over it. Apollo had issued a statement as soon as the first rumours had gathered momentum, informing the public that she'd taken an assumed name to escape publicity. There was still some speculation about them, but at least other, more important news was now starting to take precedence.

What he'd hoped was that, as the rumours ceased, his need for her would also cease. That he'd become tired of her, that the endless, aching desperation and obsession with her would fade, that his fury would fade along with it, and yet...

He couldn't stop looking at her, couldn't stop the response of his body to her, and something in his chest wouldn't stop aching. He wanted be angry with her still, but the fierceness of that fire seemed to have burned itself out, leaving only glowing embers behind.

Anger wouldn't help him anyway. Anger wouldn't help the ache or the need or the hunger. It wouldn't help the sense of betrayal that had cut to the heart of him. Being cold to her had only left him feeling hollow inside, as if in shutting her out, he was shutting out some vital part of himself that he needed for his very existence.

For the first time since that night in Hong Kong, Apollo tried to see her without the red haze of anger, and sort through what she'd told him.

Was it the truth, what she'd said about her parents? About how she'd lost everything? Or was it simply a tissue of lies to gain his sympathy? And all these protestations of love… Were they lies too? Did she mean it? She wanted him, oh, he knew that for certain, because her body didn't lie, but love?

Well, he knew about love. He knew how it blinded you, how it stopped you from seeing the truth. After all, it had blinded him to the truth about his father, had made him believe all the lies Stavros had fed him.

If she loves you, then she's blinded too. She won't see your faults.

That was true, and he had many of them. He was, after all, his father's son, and it was him who had led her father to his death. She must see that. She'd told him she was angry about the choices her father had made, but if he hadn't been around, her father would never have made those choices in the first place.

Slowly, Flora turned around, her dark, grey gaze meeting his. She was pale, her hands still clasped tightly in front of her, but she didn't flinch from him.

'There,' she said. 'I've told you everything about me. Those are the reasons I did what I did, but they're for your information only. They're not meant as justifications.' She took another breath. 'I'm sorry that I made you lie. I'm sorry I took you in. I'm sorry I turned you into your father, but I'm not sorry that I fell in love with you.' She lifted her chin in that determined way, because after all, she was a very determined woman. 'You'll never be him, Apollo. Everything you do, everything you are, is his polar opposite. You're kind, protective and you care. I was stupid not to have seen that earlier. I let my anger blind me, but… It was love that made me see who you truly are. The most amazing man I've ever met.'

He hadn't expected that, just as he didn't expect the glow in those lovely grey eyes of hers. The glow of conviction. She believed what she'd said. She wasn't lying to him now. She believed every word was the truth.

His heart tightened. He hadn't known what that would mean to him, that she saw him in that way. That she didn't see the man who'd been complicit in a scheme that had brought so many people to ruin. The man who'd believed his father's lies, who'd let love blind him to the truth.

'I know you believe that,' he said. 'But you're wrong, Flora. It's got nothing to do with anger. I loved my father, and that love blinded me to who he really was. A charlatan and a fraud. And I think it's blinding you to who I really am too, because I'm none of those things.'

He expected her to turn away, but she didn't. Instead she took a step forward, then another, slowly crossing the distance between them, until she was standing right in front of him. 'I loved my father too, and I felt the same way about him when he died. It felt like a betrayal. As if love had blinded me too, but now… I think that's wrong. Love is making me see clearly for the first time.' She tilted her head back and looked straight at him, then she reached up and put a cool palm against his cheek. 'You're all of those things, Apollo. I know you don't think you can trust me and I understand why. But you need to trust this, trust what I'm saying right now. You gave me the happiest two weeks of my life, and if that's all I ever have—'

'I killed your father, Flora,' he interrupted hoarsely. 'You can't excuse—'

'No.' Her voice was firm, and very certain, as her thumb brushed along his cheekbone. 'You didn't kill him. You told me in Hong Kong that he made a choice, and you're right. He did. I thought it was a selfish choice, and it caused me a lot of grief, a lot of heartache, but… I loved him. And maybe he thought that was his only option. I don't know. But what I do know is that I can't do anything about it now, neither of us can.'

'If I hadn't—'

'Don't, please,' she interrupted once again, though this time her voice was gentle. 'Don't do that yourself. Don't take the blame for what Dad did. You were young, and you wanted to please your father, and you didn't know what Stavros was doing.'

Her touch on his cheek was soft, tender. He'd missed that touch. He'd missed it so much. 'I should have known... I should have seen it.'

'No, you shouldn't. Like I said, you were young and—'

'I wasn't young with you.'

Regret settled on her delicate face like a weight. 'You weren't to know that either. You employed me, and you trusted me, and I broke that trust in the worst way possible. You'll never know how sorry I am for it.'

She was sorry, he could see that now. There was something in her eyes, something that looked like...hope.

'Why are you looking at me like that?' he couldn't help but ask.

'I thought you'd walk away, I thought you wouldn't listen to me, but...you stayed.' She took a breath, then dropped her hand. 'You're a better person than I'll ever be.'

A better person... He wasn't, he knew that, but she'd said all of that was in the past and there was nothing they could do about it now.

His father was dead and so was hers.

And she loved him...she *loved* him...

Was it true what she said about anger and love? Was it anger that blinded you? Was it love that made you see clearly?

Deep in his heart, Apollo felt something shift, begin to uncurl, to stretch out. To bloom.

He had lived in his own anger for a long time, had made it his familiar. It dogged him everywhere, at his heels wherever he went. It had made him make an effigy of his name and reputation, yet one made of glass that could shatter at the slightest breath. It was rigid and unbending. Unforgiving...

Flora had left that anger behind. It was obvious from the open and honest way she looked at him, letting him see everything in a way she'd never done before. Letting him see her vulnerability, her soul.

Was it that easy? And did he want to do the same? Could he lay his own anger at his father and himself aside? Was it worth it? And if he did, what would be there instead?

Apollo lifted a hand before he could stop himself, pulling an end of one of the ties holding her dress up, and then the other. The soft white cotton fell slowly from her body and she made no effort to stop it, simply looked up at him, the dark charcoal of her gaze clear and open.

She was naked beneath the cotton, her body still every bit as lovely as it had been the first time he'd seen it, her skin honeyed and golden in the sun.

'Apollo,' she murmured, lifting her arms to him, and he needed no more invitation than that. He got rid of his own towel and then, because after all there was still a piece of him that wanted to punish her a little bit more, he picked her up and took them both into the cool water of the pool.

She gasped and when he pulled her into his arms,

pressing her back against the pool wall, she twined her legs around his waist as if she'd been doing it all her life.

'Apollo,' she repeated breathlessly as he looked into her eyes, watching the familiar flame of desire leap high.

She was wet and slippery and he was too, and he thought he could probably look into her eyes for ever, watching them darken in response to her desire, and his.

She'd left behind her anger. Admitted her pain. Had come to him and apologised for what she'd done, and he believed her. Her regret was real.

But he had a choice to make. He could either let his anger and hurt win, shut her out for ever, believe her to be a con woman, the way his father had been a con-man. Or...he could let the past go. Let his father go, let his anger go.

You know what's there, underneath all of that. You know.

Perhaps he did know. And perhaps it had been there for longer than he'd cared to admit. This obsession with her, this need for her... It wasn't only physical. It had *never* been only physical. It was far more than that, it went deeper...

'I have never believed in love, *matia mou*,' he murmured, brushing kisses over her forehead and nose, the petal softness of her cheek, and then, finally, her mouth. 'I always thought it was a lie. It made you blind. Told you things that weren't true.'

'I don't care if you don't feel the same way,' she said huskily. 'I just want you.'

Apollo kissed her for a long time, then he lifted his

mouth, positioned himself and thrust inside her, easily, naturally. She moaned softly, shuddering against the pool wall.

'Tell me,' he whispered against her mouth. 'Tell me everything about you.'

He didn't make it easy for her, with the insistent press of his hips against her, but she tried, he'd give her that. Telling him about her lonely childhood and how she'd always longed for siblings. How after her father had died, she'd pass the time when her mother was out by reading anything she could get her hands on. She didn't flinch about her quest for revenge, and answered every question he asked without protest.

The gentle thrusting he was doing as she submitted to his questioning might have had something to do with that, but there was no denying her honesty.

She held back nothing.

And somewhere, in the pleasure that gripped them both, Apollo let go of his past, let go of his guilt and, most important of all, his anger, because he knew what lay under all of those things, and it was wonderful.

It turned out that Flora was right. It was surprisingly easy to let go of all those things, and once he had, he could see truly for the first time in his life.

This was what he wanted. Them, together. Flora in his arms. Flora as his wife. Flora as his future. It had never been his reputation or his good name. It had never been the accolades and nominations, all the awards and good press.

It began and ended with her.

And once he'd let love fill his heart, a powerful tide sweeping all his preconceptions and certainties aside, he could see the new landscape that it made. And it was beautiful. A new certainty. One to build a life on.

'Your turn,' she said, her voice breathless and gasping. 'Tell me everything about you.'

But by then it was becoming impossible to think, so he only took her mouth as the climax gripped her, muffling her scream of release. Then he was following her, and this time he pressed his forehead to hers, looking into her eyes as the pleasure detonated inside him.

'Oh, *matia mou*,' he murmured roughly, when he could speak. 'I was wrong about love. You're right, it doesn't blind. It doesn't lie. It helps me see the truth.'

Her breathing was starting to slow, but her grip on him didn't loosen. 'What truth?'

He looked into her eyes. 'That I love you.'

She stilled, shock rippling over her lovely face. 'What?'

'I can either stay angry at you for ever, or I can let it go.' He leaned forward and kissed her softly. 'So I'm choosing to let it go. I'm choosing to trust you. I'm choosing to love you, Flora Constantinides.'

He didn't need anything else, in that moment, because in that moment he knew.

All he'd ever needed was her.

EPILOGUE

"'APOLLO AND FLORA'S baby joy!'"

'Baby joy?' Flora looked at her husband as he began to read aloud from the magazine article underneath the headline. 'Really?'

It was a photo spread Apollo had approved, of them and their new baby. One last, final bow to the media. At least, that was what Apollo had promised her.

His green eyes glinted with a wicked humour. 'Certainly. We have a baby and it is joyous, correct?'

Flora looked down at said baby, the newly minted Elena Laura Constantinides, and smiled, her heart full of the most intense, almost painful love. 'Yes,' she said. 'Yes, that's true.'

Apollo put down the magazine and came over to where his wife sat on the couch with Elena in her arms, sitting down beside her. He bent and kissed the top of his new daughter's head, then he kissed his wife. 'You know what else is true?' he asked, settling back in the couch, an arm around Flora so she and their baby were nestled against him.

Flora glanced up at him, into his jungle green eyes,

every part of her thrilling to his presence. She smiled. 'Tell me.' It was a little ritual they had.

'That I love you,' he said, and gave her his beautiful, amazing smile.

'And I love you too,' she said, because she always had and she always would.

Love was the bedrock that they'd built their lives upon.

No word of a lie.

* * * * *

Were you captivated by Newlywed Enemies?
*Then you're certain to love these other
intensely emotional stories
by Jackie Ashenden!*

Enemies at the Greek Altar
Spanish Marriage Solution
Italian Baby Shock
The Twins That Bind
Boss's Heir Demand

Available now!

HARLEQUIN
Reader Service

Enjoyed your book?

Try the perfect subscription for Romance readers and get more great books like this delivered right to your door.

See why over 10+ million readers have tried Harlequin Reader Service.

Start with a Free Welcome Collection with free books and a gift—valued over $20.

Choose any series in print or ebook.
See website for details and order today:

TryReaderService.com/subscriptions